Praise for

Incredibly engaging banter with fun characters, and personality spilling off the page ... It was the alien buddy road trip I didn't know I needed!

Raquel Brown, RevPit Editor

Fast, fun, and funny sci-fi, done just right

Jonathan Nevair, sci-fi author, 'Wind Tide' series

Another fantastic outing from one of the rising stars of lighthearted British sci-fi... Not so much 'The Wrong Stop,' as very much the right one

KDS, book reviewer

A hilarious first-contact story... filled with wry humour, laddish banter, and many laugh out loud moments

Sue Bavey, book blogger at Sue's Musings

THE WRONG STOP

Also by Rex Burke

Odyssey Earth series

Orphan Planet

Twin Landing

Star Bound

SciFi adventures

The Wrong Stop

Third Loch from the Sun

THE WRONG STOP

A SciFi Caper

REX BURKE

Copyright © 2024 by Rex Burke

All rights reserved.

ISBN: 978-1-916694-05-7

No part of this book may be reproduced in any form or by any electronic or mechanical means, including information storage and retrieval systems, without written permission from the author, except for the use of brief quotations in a book review.

Cover design and map: Chris Hudson Design, chrishudsondesign.co.uk

Acknowledgements: A thousand thanks to my wonderful beta-readers, Sue Bavey, Lisa Rose Wright, Val Poore, Karl Forshaw and BlueSmoke Bob. Cultural consultants Foxton Brown and ShotGunKev helped out with some great insults and fake film titles. And I'm indebted, as always, to Elaine, my first reader and greatest fan.

For Elaine, my right stop

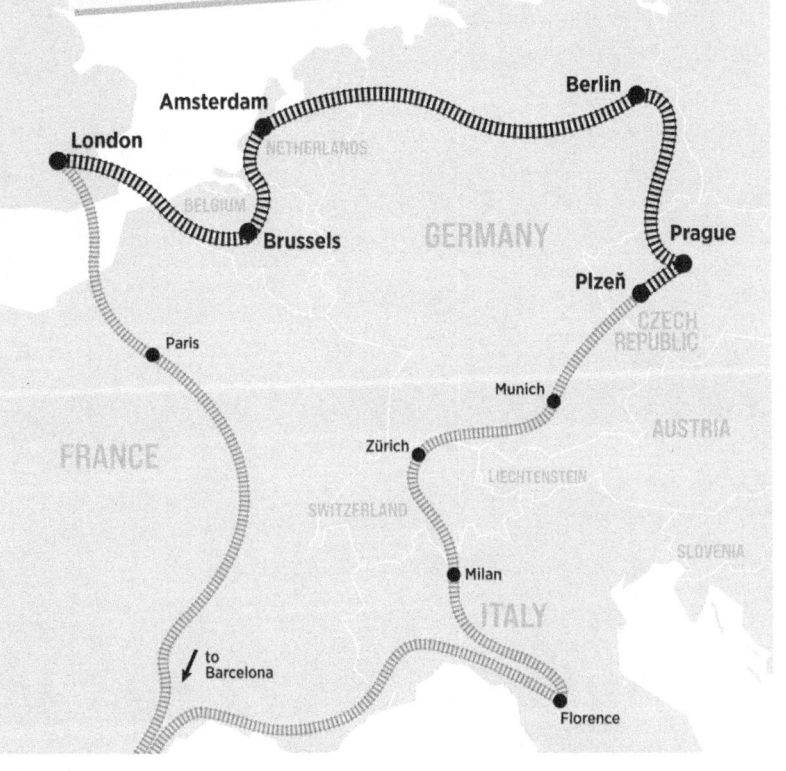

Hutch, Sully & Jed European rail tour!

Hutch
- ✓ Museums & galleries
- ✗ Talking to strangers

Sully
- ✓ Pubs, clubs & bars
- ✗ Getting up early

Jed
- ✓ WiFi connection
- ✗ Going outside

Berlin
Amsterdam
NETHERLANDS
London
BELGIUM
Brussels
GERMANY
Prague
Plzeň
CZECH REPUBLIC
Paris
Munich
AUSTRIA
Zürich
LIECHTENSTEIN
FRANCE
SWITZERLAND
SLOVENIA
Milan
ITALY
↙ to Barcelona
Florence

Prologue

From the Interrail website:
'One train pass that helps you open doors to new destinations, cultures and friendships all over Europe. Meet locals and other travellers – get ready for the adventure of a lifetime!'

Extract from the financial accounts of the Treasurers of Athena, dated 434 BC:
'We, the Treasurers of the sacred items of Athena, record the gift of two bracelets of gold offered by a visiting foreigner named [inscription unclear]. Let the nature of these treasures be inscribed on stone, and the records and treasures kept on the Acropolis in the rear chamber of the Parthenon.'

. . .

[The Treasurers of Athena were members of a guild responsible for the money, gifts and offerings kept in the temple known as the Parthenon, on the hill of the Acropolis in Athens, Greece.

Their accounts were inscribed on marble tablets, and indicate the lavish wealth once stored in the building, though all the valuable items themselves have been lost over the centuries. Except, of course, for the two famous gold bracelets (the so-called 'Elgin Bands'), referred to in the best-known of the ancient treasurers' records.

The bracelets were discovered and removed in 1801 by Lord Elgin, along with the renowned marble sculptures from the Parthenon itself.]

Chapter 1

The craft tore through the dark night skies of an alien planet, trailing a plume from the breach in the hull caused by the failure of the drive system.

Flares and sparks flew as it butted headlong through the atmosphere, while the on-board intelli-help made a million simultaneous calculations in an attempt to slow the craft's descent and regain some control.

Levelling out over a canopy of native trees, the craft deployed its ground-range sensors to plot a landing course that would result in the least possible structural damage. There was bound to be some destruction of native flora and fauna – it couldn't be helped – but as the most recent planetary review had suggested a low level of development, this wasn't a major consideration.

With an optimal trajectory set, the intelli-help deployed the servos, steadying the craft for its final approach. It buzzed the tops of the higher trees, shattering branches as it ploughed forward and down, before cutting a wide swathe through dense boughs and dull earth.

Sample-sensors checked exterior bio-levels, even as the craft ground on through the trees. When it finally came to a halt, banked slightly on one side but otherwise still largely intact, the intelli-help had already determined that the local conditions were suitable. More or less, anyway. You wouldn't want to live here, but you could cope with the conditions if you had to.

That just left the small matter of emergency extraction.

In this remote arm of the galaxy, there was no point in broadcasting an alert – there was no one remotely equipped to help for several light years. And, in fact, advertising a presence on this planet was not a good idea, if previous shared experience was anything to go by.

The intelli-help scanned the files and pulled the relevant records. At least there was an option, though it was going to require some local knowledge and a fair amount of luck.

More files were scanned, and a brief search of planetary networks instigated to acquire the necessary background data. The intelli-help ran its searches behind a firewall, just to be on the safe side. Early-stage development, maybe, but still best to exercise caution on this planet if extraction was going to be successful.

It took a few more moments to prepare the presentation – mapping, logistics, camouflage, protection, resources – and then the intelli-help was finished. It had done its job; it could do no more.

The craft wouldn't fly again. Even the most cursory of post-landing scans had confirmed what it already knew. Unexplained but catastrophic failure of the drive system. The intelli-help added a note to that effect, for completeness' sake.

For security reasons, it decoupled itself from the craft's single passenger. A fully sentient being would have said that that felt like a small death. For the intelli-help, it was everything and nothing.

It could wait here on this planet forever if required, untethered, dormant. Someone would come again to reconnect, or they wouldn't. In the great scheme of things – figure of speech, there was no scheme – it hardly mattered.

Now the intelli-help turned its attention to life support. The tank had been compromised, but not fatally. There was still time.

As the craft powered down, it directed resources to where they were needed, and discharged the harmful emissions already creeping in through the breached hull.

The intelli-help ran diagnostics, checked the levels and primed the bio-boosters. It scanned the presentation one last time, knowing it was complete – knowing that what happened next would be out of its hands. Another figure of speech. Out of its control.

Then, finally, it cracked the auto-locks on the tank and initiated the revival sequence.

Time to wake them up and wish them luck. They were going to need it.

BBC World News report:

'And finally, inhabitants of Plzeň, in western Bohemia in the Czech Republic, were disturbed late last night by an unexplained display of lights. Our correspondent reports:'

"Yes, thank you. As you say, many observers reported the phenomenon, as dramatic streaks and flashes lit up the night sky above this historic medieval town. An eyewitness recorded the scene on their phone and it made for quite a show.

[*Video plays – scene of revellers in an old-town square; shouts as lights flash quickly overhead; car alarms and barking dogs. Camera follows the trail, shakily, until the lights disappear into the distance a few seconds later.*]

Local police were inundated with calls, and investigations remain ongoing, but so far there has been no explanation for the sudden appearance – and disappearance – of the lights.

A spokesperson for the Czech aviation authority said that there had been no diversions or other incidents concerning flights into and out of nearby airports. Meanwhile, military authorities have declined to comment on the possibility of night-time aerial-combat training over the town.

Which leaves many inhabitants asking – were the

lights perhaps evidence of a close encounter with a UFO? Some of the people we spoke to last night certainly thought so [*video plays – boisterous people, variously singing, chanting and pointing at the sky*], but there may be a simpler explanation.

Since 1842, Plzeň – or Pilsen, in English – has been the home of the famous pale lager beer known as Pils. Did these young people see the lights of an alien craft in the skies of the Czech Republic? Or had they simply enjoyed the hospitality of Plzeň's friendly bars and cafés just a little too much?

Some I spoke to last night are sure that the truth is out there. Others, though, think that the answer lies in the bottom of one of these. [*Reporter raises large glass of beer and smiles to camera*]

And now, back to the studio."

Chapter 2

"On a scale of one to ten," said Sully. "One is, you didn't have anything to drink last night. Ten is basically dead."

"Nine, then," said Hutch, whose head felt like it was being worked over with a hammer from the inside, by a little man who kept belching into his mouth. A little man who had apparently been eating sardines.

"Maybe an eight?" said Jed. "Probably a nine if I open my eyes."

"Lightweights," said Sully. "I'm going to go and see if the bar's open. Get us a refreshing breakfast beverage."

That was Sully all over. Hutch had known him since they were both seven years old, in Miss Potter's junior class. Old Ma Potty, they called her – seemed ancient to them, she'd have probably been twenty-five.

From seven to fifteen, Sully had just been Sully. Good fun, always there, best friend. From sixteen onwards, he'd been Sully-Plus – the plus being alcohol, mostly beer, but you know, whatever – and he was still good-fun-best-friend material, but it was exhausting for anyone with a normal metabolism.

Put it this way, the refreshing breakfast beverage wasn't going to be coffee. And if it was, it would have something else in it.

Jed opened his eyes, and watched Sully make his way down the aisle of the train. Then closed his eyes again. "Ugh, daylight. Knew it would be a nine," he said. "How does he do it?"

"No one's ever known," said Hutch. "He's a medical mystery. It doesn't seem to affect him. Or he's just very good at pretending not to be hungover. They'll write a thesis about him one day."

"You know it's the stuff they put in it, gives us the hangover?"

"No kidding, genius."

"Not the alcohol. Think about it. No one ever got hangovers in the olden days. Drank beer for breakfast, gin all day, whisky nightcaps, still managed to conquer the world, build an empire. But now they want the masses docile, so they put something extra in it. Keeps us dull, clouds the brain, in case we rise up against them. There's a guy on YouTube talks about it."

And that was Jed all over. There wasn't a mad theory he didn't have time for – or a mad guy on YouTube he didn't follow. There was no point asking who 'They' or 'Them' were – Jed wasn't quite in lizard-people territory, but membership of the secretive world cabal seemed to change every week according to whichever channel he'd been watching.

Jed wouldn't eat yoghurt ("because of the radiation"), rocked Pokémon T-shirts, and had a poster on his wall at home that said, 'It's all a simulation.' He was as exhausting in his own way as Sully, which was why Hutch had said, "Come on, not Jed!" when it had first been put to him.

Of the four other people they shared their student flat with, Jed was the one you wouldn't want to be stuck with in the pub, let alone in the same train carriage, on the same holiday.

"He can share the costs, it'll be cheaper," Sully had said. "Anyway, I felt sorry for him. He said he wasn't doing anything this summer, and everyone else is going away."

"He'd have been happy staying in his room — playing with his little Reddit mates, watching YouTubers cage-fight each other, whatever it is he does in there. Has he even got a passport? I don't think I've ever seen him outside the flat."

"He's not that bad. I didn't think you'd mind. Anyway, I can't take it back now. He's very excited. He says he's buying special travel trousers."

Hutch looked across at Jed, his eyes still closed, head lolling back, legs sprawled. The cargo shorts *were* ridiculous. Two sizes too big, dropping somewhere between knee and ankle, they fell in bulges like overstuffed shopping bags.

Jed reckoned that a backpack would hurt his shoul-

The Wrong Stop

ders, and that the pocket-shorts were a genius method of packing. Consequently, he only carried a small daypack and had everything else stored in one of his many zipped and buttoned pockets – toothbrush, wet wipes, headphones, boxer shorts, you name it. Whereas Hutch and Sully sported regular backpacks, like normal people.

Hutch shook his head at the idiocy, which only made him dizzy, and looked out of the train window. Bits of the Czech Republic flashed by – halfway to Prague and whatever was in store for them once they'd perked up a bit. Or had their first beer of the day, if Sully had anything to do with it.

The whole trip had been a compromise. Given three weeks travelling by train around Europe with an Interrail pass, Hutch had done his best to try and have something to show for it except monumental hangovers – hence the first two weeks doing Paris and The Louvre, Barcelona and the Sagrada Família, Florence and The Uffizi, a boat trip on Lake Como, and a cable-car ride in the Swiss Alps.

"What are we, ninety?" Sully had said, looking at the route that Hutch had planned. "We're nineteen, mate. We're students. We should be drinking fishbowls in Ayia Napa. The rugby boys are going to Ayia Napa. Why aren't we going to Ayia Napa?"

"Because there isn't a train to Ayia Napa."

"There must be. Everywhere has trains. You said we could go anywhere we wanted with this rail pass. Unlimited travel, you said."

"Do you even know where Ayia Napa is?"

"I want to say yes – "

"Cyprus. It's an island, across a whole bunch of water. We're not going to Cyprus. We're going to backpack around Europe by train. I thought you wanted to go interrailing?"

"I do, but you know – I don't want to die of boredom in the, what is it, the Uffecki – "

"Uffizi."

"Right, there, and have to be resuscitated with the kiss of life by an elderly German tourist in lederhosen, with bad breath and a twirly moustache."

"This is a very niche fear you have, Sully. You might want to consider therapy."

"All I'm saying is, if we're going for a geriatric boat ride on Lake Bore-mo, we have to do some things I want to do as well. Fun things. Normal things, preferably involving beer. And Jed agrees with me."

"Jed's giddy at the thought of being allowed out into sunlight. He doesn't care where he goes."

The compromise was the return leg to London through Munich, Prague, Berlin and Brussels – or the 'Beer Square,' as Sully proclaimed it, when he looked at the shape the cities made on the map.

"Technically, an irregular polygon," said Jed, "I'm in."

And the deal was sealed when Sully discovered that the train route from Munich to Prague happened to pass through Plzeň.

Hutch had been perplexed. "You want to spend the

night in the Czech Republic's fourth largest town, with its sixteenth-century cathedral and nineteenth-century synagogue?"

"The ignorance. You'd think Wikipedia would lead with the interesting stuff. We shall be visiting the historic Pilsner Urquell Brewery, and more specifically going on their brewery tour. Possibly more than once. And then we will get bladdered in whichever bar serves the finest Pilsner beer. Which will be all of them."

The previous day and night, consequently, had been a bit of a blur. Hutch hadn't known it was possible to get thrown out of a brewery, but every day was a school day with Sully.

The town's bars had been more accommodating and Sully had been right, the Pils beer could not be faulted. Slipped down a treat. The last thing Hutch remembered, on their way back to the hostel before they crashed for the night, was the light-show in the sky above the old town – streaks of red and white that lit up the rooftops and arced their way out into the countryside beyond.

Hutch nudged Jed's foot. "Hey, you remember that, last night? The lights?"

Jed opened his eyes and moved in his seat. Various pockets swung and rustled. "I'd say I'm gradually heading down from an eight to a seven," he said. "Lights?"

"In the sky, on our way back to the hostel."

"Lights, really? I don't remember much after Sully tried to get in that brewery vat."

"What was he thinking? He was never going to get the hatch open."

"Schoolboy error."

Right on cue, Sully appeared back at the seats carrying a tray.

"Breakfast is served, boys."

Hutch sniffed the cups warily. "That actually smells like coffee, Sully. Well done. And what are those?"

"The guy in the buffet says they're like doughnuts but better. Good for the stomach, apparently."

"Well, this is all very – "

"You eat a couple and then, he says, you have a shot of this," at which Sully brandished a flat half-bottle of something colourless with a label showing a devil with a pitchfork.

"Christ, Sully."

"He can't help you now, but never fear, Sully's here. Right, who's first?"

Chapter 3

Information acquired, they closed down the files and mothballed the intelli-help. Didn't like to abandon the craft like this – ditched on an alien planet – but there was no choice.

Crack the hatch, time to go.

Crisp air, the right side of breathable. Unidentifiable smells – presumably the local flora. Night sounds, calls, scuffles. Nothing to worry about, according to the files. Other than the one big concern, obviously. Which was why it was definitely time to leave.

Camouflage and systems check – done.

Comms integration – done.

Target destination – acquired.

On their own now, but it was going to be fine. No point thinking otherwise. Follow the protocols, and everything should work out. Always the optimist.

Light from a moon helped pick a way through a forest. Unsteady at first, getting used to the feel and balance, then quicker – distancing themselves from the craft, as they shook off the last effects of the forced landing.

First location check at the edge of the tree cover, approaching a settlement, status unknown. Plotted route was straightforward, but time-and-distance calculations were not encouraging. Going to have to co-opt local systems, and sooner rather than later.

The structure – building? – lay straight ahead. Purpose – confirmed. A corner bathed in shadows provided cover until first light. Morning. Blue skies, high white clouds, strong sun. Surprisingly warm. Quite pretty really, considering the state of the planet.

Deep breath. Step out, look straight ahead, only engage if essential. It was all going to be fine.

Final camouflage and systems check. They were as prepared as they could be. Or maybe not quite – there, those would be useful.

And finally, here it was.

Stepping on now.

———

Urgent communication (Level: Classified)
To: Director (Europe), Bureau of External Visitor Incursions (BEVI)
From: BEVI Tracking Station (Germany)

'ALERT. Observation posts at Frankfurt [23.44, Central European Summer Time] and Nuremberg [23.49] have reported an apparent entry-trigger.

The reports meet the alert criteria set out in Standing Order UAP2. There is current, credible evidence for insertion-apparent of a visitor craft in the Central European theatre. Calculations put the probability of visitor insertion-actual at 93 percent.

Tracking data showed a significant slowing of velocity above the western Bohemian border area, with contact lost in the vicinity of Plzeň. Local reports of 'lights' are beginning to emerge.

X-Team agents in Nuremberg are en route and will deploy within the hour.'

———

Urgent communication (Level: Classified)
To: Professor James Storm, Head of Operations, BEVI Research Unit (Germany)
From: Director (Europe), Bureau of External Visitor Incursions (BEVI)

'UPDATE. Insertion-actual has now been confirmed and the crash site at Plzeň secured.

Agents are still assessing the impact zone, but initial findings are remarkable – remote observations show that the craft is largely intact [*images* attached – verification code required to view].

I'm authorising full restoration of Research Unit

funding and resources. It's imperative we don't lose the time advantage our spotter posts have given us.

Given the external news reports based on eyewitness sightings, I've also authorised comms interference with our European friends. Local police and regional authorities have been supplied with a cover story, and an exclusion zone is now in force, with access to the crash site restricted from all directions.

This gives us a window to operate in, so let's make it count – as of now, the unit is back online, with full executive authority in this matter.'

[*Voice-note attached*]:

'Jim – this is the real deal, just look at the pictures! Whatever it is, and wherever it came from, I want to know.

The story should hold long enough for agents to get the craft to your guys in the research unit. Retrieval rigs are on their way – they'll get it out by road if they can, rail if not.

I don't have to tell you how huge this is. I want your best X-Team people on this – we only get one chance.

And, Jim – if there's anything in there, alive or dead, make sure you get ET locked down pronto. I'm sick of having to say pretty-please to the Americans to go and have a look at their little pal. I want one of my own, are we clear?'

Chapter 4

Sully poured another splash into his coffee, sipped it approvingly, and looked out of the train window.

"Where are we, still in Czechoslovakia?"

Jed checked his phone. "Yep. Just passing some place with no vowels and lots of zeds. Half an hour from Prague, although – " and he looked closer at the map, puzzled – "it appears to have changed its name to Praha."

"Czechoslovakia?" said Hutch. "It hasn't been called Czechoslovakia for thirty years. More, probably. Geography department still turning out our finest minds, I see."

"All right, Stephen Fry," said Sully.

"Yeah, all right ..." Jed tailed off, struggling for a retort, before coming up with "University Challenge."

Sully laughed at that, and even Hutch had to smile. "Good one," he said.

"Those lights, last night?" said Jed, turning his

phone screen to face them. "It's saying here it was a cargo plane. Mechanical failure." He checked his phone again, scanning the report. "Spilled some agricultural chemicals. They've evacuated a village."

"Dunno," said Hutch. "Cargo plane? It was going pretty fast, whatever it was."

"Well, it would be, wouldn't it? If it was just about to crash?" said Sully. "You know, gravity and all that? It would be going fast."

"Gravity! Listen to Einstein." Hutch jeered, grateful for the comeback opportunity.

"Course, they would say that," said Jed.

"Who would say what?"

"They always cover up things with a plausible story. Tell us it was a downed cargo plane, when really – "

"Let me guess. It was a UFO, which just happened to have buzzed us and then landed in a nearby field?"

"We don't say UFO. We prefer the term UAP, Unidentified Aerial Phenomenon."

"We? Who's 'we'?"

"Jed's in Nerd-Soc, aren't you, mate?" said Sully.

"Funny. Mystery-Soc. And it could have been a UAP. We'd never know, because they hush this stuff up all the time."

"You don't even remember seeing the lights!" said Hutch.

"Not the point. Anyway, I'm just saying. They've got bits of spacecraft and alien tech in all sorts of government facilities. How do you think we invented the internet?"

"Even for you, this is mad," said Hutch. "What are you talking about?"

"The internet. A sudden massive advance in what we could do with computers, and it came out of nowhere. That's because they retro-engineered the tech from an alien craft that crashed in Utah in the 1970s."

"According to a man on YouTube who lives with his mum and broadcasts from her basement in his underwear."

"You'll see," shrugged Jed. "It'll all come out one day."

"You don't have a girlfriend, do you?" said Hutch.

"No," said Jed. "What's that got to do with it?"

"Nothing, just wondered."

"A low blow, Hutch, man," said Sully. "None of us are exactly blessed in that department."

"Yeah, but we probably could get a girlfriend. If we wanted, if we could be bothered. Whereas, ET here – " and Hutch gestured at Jed, as if it was self-evident why the members of Mystery-Soc bought single-serve ready meals and arrived on their own at club nights.

"There are girls in Mystery-Soc," said Jed, defensively. "Well, one. Says she saw Bigfoot when she was doing Camp America in Texas last year. We're not sure we believe her – sightings aren't usually that far south, and the footprint was sketchy at best."

"You think it's possible that a UFO landed in the Czech Republic's beer capital, but question the veracity of a Deep South Bigfoot sighting?"

"UAP. And it's a matter of evidence."

"Like the internet?" Hutch laughed.

"Exactly. Or Velcro."

"I'm not even going to ask."

Jed pulled at one of the sticky strips on one of his many pockets. "Let's just say that this bad boy wouldn't exist if it hadn't been for what they recovered from the 1947 Jura mountain incident."

"Christ."

"You called?" Sully tipped another measure into Hutch's coffee cup, which by now was at least fifty percent not coffee.

"It's only ten o'clock, Sully."

"Exactly. A gentle pick-me up. A little livener before we get down to business in Prague. Or Praha, as our foil-hatted friend here would have it."

"And by business, you mean?"

"The finest and cheapest beers known to humanity, of course."

Hutch groaned at the thought and looked away, along the aisle of the train. A guard was making his way towards them, checking tickets as he went. He had stopped at a group of three a little way down – backpackers like them, by the looks of it, who were all reaching for their phones and opening apps.

"Guys, rail passes," said Hutch, grabbing his own phone.

They all had mobile passes, which required nothing more than entering the day's train route and showing a bar code, but even so, it was like getting toddlers ready for an outing when it came to managing Sully and Jed.

The Wrong Stop

Hutch did most of the heavy lifting with the route-planning – truth be told, he enjoyed it – but making sure they all had a valid travel pass for the train was only the half of it. Getting them to the station every day, he could have done with reins. And Hutch had never thought he'd actually have to check if anyone needed the toilet before they set off. Sully's super-charged coffee wasn't helping anyone's concentration either.

The guard had moved closer. Now he was standing three or four rows away, next to another passenger, who ignored him at first. The guard tried again, touching his shoulder, and the guy looked up.

"Tickets," said the guard in English, to another blank look from the passenger. Honestly, thought Hutch, how hard was it to have your ticket ready?

He shifted his gaze back to Sully and Jed, checking they had their phones out. Sully at least had clocked the situation. Jed, on the other hand, was busy removing items from some of the less strategically placed pockets in his cargo shorts and piling them on the table.

"Dude, Chrissake."

"Looking for my charger," he said. "I keep it in the electrical sundries pocket. Or I thought I did."

Sully snorted – something about a moron pocket. "Just show him your pass and do all that when he's gone. Idiot."

Hutch looked back. The guy down the aisle seemed to have resolved the situation. He had one hand on the guard's arm, talking to him at last, and then touched a smartwatch screen and showed it to the guard.

A minute later, the guard was with the three of them – a slight askance look at the almost empty bottle of forty-percent hooch, as he checked their passes. Sully met his gaze, and raised a coffee cup to him in a toast.

And then it was back to watching Jed, who was gradually filling the table with an improbable selection of items – laundry pegs, bandages, a sink plug, Yorkshire teabags – as he searched for his charger.

"There you are," he said happily. "In the snacks and vitamins pocket," he explained, as if that was an entirely normal thing to say.

Two weeks of this so far, thought Hutch. The same rigmarole every morning, without fail. At least on this occasion Jed hadn't excavated the rancid underwear pocket. That was a day the security officer at The Uffizi would never forget.

At Prague – "Oh, right, Praha," said Jed, "I get it" – the station concourse was filled with people, and they picked their way through the crowd, backpacks bumping occasionally. Jed clanked along behind Hutch and Sully, his well-stocked shorts swinging with the weight.

Towards the exit, the crowd funnelled into a line, and everyone shuffled forward, a few feet at a time.

"Plod," said Sully, nodding his head over at a group of cops on the periphery, scanning the arriving passengers. There were more at the main station entrance, as well as a couple of dark-suited guys with earpieces talking animatedly while looking into the mid-distance.

"Wonder what all that's for?"

"They've heard Jed's in town. Never seen a human made out of pockets before."

"Velcro Man."

"The Walking Supermarket."

"Swiss Army Idiot."

"Bog off," said Jed.

"All right, Oscar Wilde, keep your shorts on."

Chapter 5

Voice recording, Plzeň site, Czech Republic:

X-Team agent
- Yeah, Prof, can confirm, hatch is open. Awaiting instruction.

Head of Operations, BEVI Research Unit
[response unavailable]

- Yes, a hatch. No visible outer lock or mechanism. But it's definitely open. Or rather, been opened.

[response unavailable]

- OK, understood. Safety first. Checking now.
Scanning.
[pause]
- Heat scars, as expected. Readings nominal at

entrance. No organic or biological trace detected. Drone-cam deployed. It's clearing the threshold now and – whoa!

[response unavailable]

- I know, it's just – when you see it, you'll get it. Check your feed. It's what you've always wanted. This was – is – a manned craft.

[response unavailable]

- Personnel, occupied, inhabited, whatever.

[response unavailable]

- Because there's what looks like a life-support tank in there, that's why! Kind of a Perspex tube? Maybe ten feet long, supports at either end, some fluid on the floor.
[pause]

[response unavailable]

- Yeah, sorry. We lost the video feed. What can I say, don't send a drone to do a field agent's job. I'll have to go in if you want to see any more.

[response unavailable]

- Well, too late for that. We haven't got a spare, anyway. I'm already halfway in. Hang on.
[pause]
- Bigger inside than it looks on the feed. A lot bigger. I'm approaching the tank now. Seems intact.
[pause]
- Actually, maybe not. There's a crack down one side – hence the fluid, I suppose. And I can see a panel inside – looks like a touchscreen? – but it's dark. No power. Sending images now. You got them?

[response unavailable]

- You want me to open it? You sure? OK, if you say so, Prof. What's the worst that could happen?

[response unavailable]

- Very funny. I notice you're holed up in your nice little research unit, while I do all the actual alien hunting. Right, opening it now. Trying to, anyway.
[pause]

[response unavailable]
[response unavailable]

- All right, keep your hair on. It's not that easy. Turns out it's spring-loaded, I've had to prop it open. You want the good news or the bad news?

[response unavailable]

- Right, well, the good news is, we're not alone. In the universe, I mean. Not that I thought we were, given our line of work. Just nice to see some hard evidence for a change.

[response unavailable]

- Focus, right. Well, this is definitely a life-support system – some kind of cryo-tank. There's a six- or seven-foot-long tray in here, headrest at one end, plenty of room for a big guy. Detachable face-helmet, swing-arm monitor. Partially flooded – sort of a liquid gel, I'm sampling it now. You can test it back at the lab.

[response unavailable]

- Well, it didn't melt my glove, let's put it like that.

[response unavailable]

- That's the bad news, Prof. There's nowhere to hide in here, and no mangled alien body. ET's not home. You seeing the body-shaped depression in the tray on the images? Reckon he – it, they – popped the tank when the ship crashed, and scarpered.

[response unavailable]

- We'll start with the immediate area. But it's the middle of the night, and this is a big forest. With a massive scorch mark through it now, and bits of trees everywhere. It's going to take some time.

[response unavailable]

- I get it. Urgent. Top secret, all that. I'm getting the team on it as fast as I can. Matey can't have got far. And their spaceship is pretty banged up, so they might be too. That would slow them down, if they're on foot.

[response unavailable]

- I wish you hadn't said that. I just sort of assumed they'd have feet. You don't pay me enough for this, Prof.

Chapter 6

"Really?" Hutch looked doubtful.

"I'm in," said Jed.

"Come on, grandad," said Sully. "It'll be fun."

"It's not what you'd call cultural, though, is it?" said Hutch, as they dumped their bags in the hostel and waited for Jed to empty his pockets. "I feel we should do something first, before getting wasted again."

"That's just where you're wrong. It's not getting wasted. It's a fusion of modern concepts and ancient practices."

"You're reading that off the website. It's a spa."

"I think you are missing the point, Hutch, mate. It is a beer spa. Where else in the world can you do this? We can literally sit in warm, bubbly beer – which is a hundred-percent natural, by the way, they're very keen on that – in handmade oak tubs."

"And drink cold Czech lager. Unlimited amounts of cold Czech lager."

"You have correctly identified the unique and authentic nature of this attraction, Jed, yes. What could be more cultural?"

"I suppose that does sound quite nice." Hutch flexed his shoulders. He ached like hell, after a night in a hostel bunk bed and a morning enduring a ferocious hangover on a train.

"That's my boy! I promise, you are not going to be on your deathbed, wishing you'd gone to more contemporary art galleries and interpretive dance shows. No, you will gather your nearest and dearest around you and tell them of the time that Uncle Sully took you to a beer spa in Prague. We will weep together at the memory, and then you will slip away into the abyss, with a smile on your lips, while I take them all to the pub to toast your memory."

"It's touching that you think you'll still be alive, hanging around my deathbed. You'll be long gone – medical science will have had those organs out of you years before. There'll probably be a condition named after you."

"Are we going or what?" said Jed, who had been busy removing items of clothing while ferreting around in his belongings. He turned to face them. "Swimming stuff, right?"

There was a stunned silence, as they took in the spectacle.

"My eyes!" said Sully. "Make it stop."

"What in God's name are you wearing?"

"My swimmers. Trunks."

Jed stood in front of them in a tight-fitting Day-Glo garment that was all right for a bout in the ring with Mack 'The Hammer' McGee but entirely wrong for swimming, or even for sitting in beer.

It started below the knees, snugly highlighted the bits of Jed in the middle that you really didn't want highlighted, and finished somewhere under his armpits. There was a pocket on the chest – what else? – with the ensemble completed by a pair of steampunk-style goggles that Jed was currently wearing high on his forehead.

He looked like a really crap children's party entertainer, possibly one featured on a 'Wanted' poster.

Hutch and Sully laughed long and loud.

"Dude, you're not wearing that. They'll call the police."

"They'll call the local high-security sex-offender unit, see if anyone's escaped."

"I have to," said Jed. "I have delicate skin. I get sunburned."

"It's inside, genius. Sitting in a tub of beer. You might get drunk skin, if you stay in long enough. You're not going to get sunburned."

"Suppose. I could wear my spare pair of shorts instead?"

"Don't tell me, you keep your spare shorts in one of your main shorts' pockets? And what's in the pockets of your spare pair of shorts? The mind boggles."

"Wear what you want. Just don't ever produce that thing again. Where did you even get it?"

"One of the guys in Mystery-Soc lent the swimsuit to me. The goggles are mine."

"Why doesn't any of that surprise us?"

As it happened, the beer spa turned out to be a hit, exactly as advertised – warm-beer jacuzzi, unlimited cold pints – and they spent a couple of hours taking the edge off the day.

It was all a bit last-days-of-Rome – sitting in a frothy hot tub, being brought lagers by young women dressed on the wench side of waitress. But Hutch supposed that the last days of Rome were probably quite nice, until the barbarians came in through the door with clubs and maces. Either way, the success rather emboldened Sully, who now fancied himself as the holiday's cultural director.

"I don't know what all the fuss has been about, Hutch. With your little spreadsheets and lists. How hard is it to organise a bit of sightseeing? There's a Beer Museum, let's do that next."

"Of course there is."

"You wanted museums."

"Is there anything in Prague that isn't to do with beer?"

"An unusual request, but let's see. Ah, now then, this will do the trick. The Sex Machines Museum."

"You're making that up."

"I am not, see for yourself."

Hutch looked over Sully's shoulder at the screen. There was, it seemed, such a place. How had it come to this, the Baroque city of Mozart and Kafka? The historic capital of Bohemia, residence of the Holy Roman Emperor?

"Jed? I can't quite believe I'm saying this, but do you want to see some sex machines?"

"Why not?"

"Don't be turning up in your gimpy swimsuit, they'll think you're an exhibit."

"Sod off."

Later, Hutch did at least persuade the pair of them to walk over the Charles Bridge and back, pushing through throngs of tourists for a riverside view of Prague. Sully conceded that it was "all right for a bridge" and Jed took a selfie of them all in front of one of the statues. A jazz band in the middle of the bridge played for the crowd, while puppeteers manipulated dancing skeletons for tips.

After which, Hutch thought he'd wrung as much cultural tolerance out of Sully as he was going to, and they wound their way through the cobbled back streets to an old pub they'd found on TripAdvisor.

"See," said Sully. "Prague. Beer. Pubs. I told you this was a good idea."

And it was, sitting around benches in a tree-shaded courtyard, as generously moustachioed waiters brought round schooner after schooner of home-brewed ale that, according to Sully, was as good as free – if he'd understood the exchange rate properly.

"They do sausages," said Jed, excitedly, at some point, which was about the last thing that Hutch remembered, when he woke up the next morning with the sun blaring through unshaded windows in the hostel dorm.

There were whimpers, grunts and snores from half a dozen others in the bunk beds around him – for one horrible minute, Hutch thought he'd woken up in the Sex Machines Museum – and he checked for Sully and Jed. Present, if not entirely correct, given the sounds and smells coming from that part of the room.

Bloody Sully. Thank God they only had a few more days of this. Not for the first time, Hutch wondered how he did it. They had literally bathed in beer, and then applied more of it internally – not forgetting the sausages – and yet Sully would be as right as rain. While Hutch felt like his brain had been removed with a rusty saw.

Right now, though, Sully was fast asleep and snoring, which wouldn't do at all, so Hutch took great delight in poking him awake.

"Berlin, remember? Time to roll."

They made it to the station with half an hour to spare, passing through a line of local police at the main entrance. Inside, on the concourse, there was more visible security – uniformed station employees in conversation with a group of men in flak jackets and camo caps.

One moved his head as the three of them walked past, his eyes following Jed and his voluminous pockets for a while, before snapping his attention back to the group. Sully saw it and grinned.

"You can see why they'd be interested in you. As a

rule, drug mules usually swallow or insert their stash. Not, you know, wear it."

"Yeah, Jed, you could offer to make them a cup of tea from the appliances pocket."

"Sod off, both of you. Wonder what they're here for, though?"

"There's been an alarming sighting of an alien in a leotard, apparently. It's terrified the locals."

"Yeah, Star-Dork."

"The Gimp Who Fell to Earth."

"Close Encounters of the Nerd Kind."

"Invasion of the Pocket-Snatchers."

"2001: A Space Idiocy."

Hutch and Sully traded improv insults while Jed studiously ignored them, scanning the departures board above their heads.

"There," he said, "that's our train, the 10.25. And it's not a leotard, it's a swimsuit – " and then the rest of his reply was drowned out by a loud station announcement.

Chapter 7

Announcement, Praha Hlavni (Prague Main Station):

'Attention, all passengers, this is a security warning. Please keep your belongings with you at all times, and note that you are only allowed on the station concourse if you have a valid travel ticket.

Spot checks are being carried out today – please assist our staff and other authorities in their duties by presenting your travel documents if requested. Thank you for your cooperation, and have a pleasant journey.'

Urgent communication (Level: Classified)
To: Director (Europe), Bureau of External Visitor Incursions (BEVI)
From: Professor James Storm, Head of Operations, BEVI Research Unit (Germany)

'Chief – X-Team agents report a single live asset (designated 'Matey'), whereabouts unknown. Possibly injured. Efforts to obtain are currently under way.

Initial investigation of the craft suggests Matey is humanoid, though we've got no more information than that at the moment – the techs are still working on site.

We're moving the craft back here as soon as possible – even on its own, this is hugely significant. We've never had a piece of hardware this big before. This changes everything.

Matey appears to be on the move, but we've got everything and everyone on the ground. This looks like a crash, not a controlled landing, and there's nowhere for Matey to go. It's only a matter of time.'

Chapter 8

"It isn't my fault," said Hutch. "The app said you didn't need seat reservations."

They stood bunched inside by the doors, as the Berlin train pulled away from Prague station. The carriage they had just walked through was packed – not an empty seat in sight. The one in front of them looked exactly the same, and they weren't the only passengers standing with their bags and looking forlornly at the smug, seated gits who hadn't taken any notice of the app and had reserved a seat.

"Dining car," said Sully. "There'll be seats in there. And drinks."

The dining car was three more carriages down – all full – and on first sight there didn't seem to be any available seats there either.

"Three beers?" said Sully, hopefully, standing at the buffet counter. "Might as well make the best of it."

The Wrong Stop

"To drink, you must sit." The waiter gestured down the carriage. "No seat, no drink."

There was one table halfway down with four seats, occupied by a single passenger sitting by the window. They slid in apologetically after hoisting their backpacks in the rack above.

"Do you mind if we – ?" said Sully.

The seat occupant – young bloke, early twenties – turned and looked blankly at him.

"Sorry," said Hutch. "It's OK?" He pointed at the three of them and at the spare seats, as Jed plonked himself down next to the stranger, with Sully opposite. The guy gave them another blank look and then turned to gaze out of the window.

"Guess so." Sully rubbed his hands at the approach of the waiter. "Right then gentlemen, as we were. Beers – Pils – *bitte*."

"To drink, you must eat."

"I thought it was sitting?"

"Yes. Also eating." The waiter tapped his notepad.

"And no more requirements after that? No more beer-related restrictions?"

"Sully, leave the man alone. We don't want to get thrown out, there's nowhere else to sit."

"I'm just saying. There seem to be a lot of transportation bye-laws regarding the sale of beer."

"Well, don't. We'll have – Jed, what do you want?"

"Sausages?"

"Really? Again? Go on then. Sausages." Hutch

searched for the word – "*Bratwurst?*" – and gestured around the table. "And chips? *Frites?*"

"And beers," said Sully. "I miss the old days. When was it – oh, yes, yesterday – when you could have a drink on a train without having to fill in a questionnaire."

The waiter gave Sully a stern look before leaving, returning five minutes later with four plates and four beers. He'd gone before anyone had realised his mistake, and Hutch would have got up to call him back, but Sully intervened, commandeering the extra beer for himself.

"If it's a Tuesday in July, and you don't have a doctor's note, you're probably only allowed one beer on a German train. I'm not risking it."

"And I'm having the sausage," said Jed, "for later." He wrapped it in a napkin and found a place for it in one of his nether pockets.

"Jesus," said Hutch. "I wouldn't mind, except that won't be the worst thing in those pockets. I heard rustling earlier."

"It's the airmail envelopes," said Jed. "I can't get them to lie straight."

"Said the entirely normal person about his entirely normal pocket contents. Envelopes? What's wrong with WhatsApp? What are you, some nineteenth-century gentleman traveller?"

"I don't use electronic-based communications, they can hack into those."

"Don't ask," said Sully, as he saw Hutch start to mouth, "They?"

"I really don't think GCHQ are going to be that bothered by your holiday letters to your mum. I'm assuming they're to your mum. Or is it Sully's mum?"

"Your mum," said Jed. "Anyway, it's not GCHQ you have to worry about. This YouTube channel – "

"Jesus. Not this again."

"Sorry about him," said Sully, over the table to the stranger, who was still staring out of the window. "I know what he looks like, but he's harmless really."

"Sod off."

"Very limited vocabulary. The doctors say it's the medication."

Jed moved to remonstrate with Sully and the stranger turned in his seat to look at him for the first time. And then looked across at Sully, who was addressing him again.

"Anyway, apologies. For busting in on you here as well. Would you like some chips?" He gestured at the spare plate, now minus its sausage.

The stranger looked at the plate as Sully took a swig from his beer.

"Cheeps," he said, in a soft voice.

"Chips, fries, *pommes frites*. Yours if you want them, we've got plenty." Sully picked up a chip off his own plate and ate it, and then another, which he brandished over the table. "Honestly, least we can do, for, you know – " and he nodded at Jed, who scowled.

"Cheeps," said the guy again. Light T-shirt showing

under a zipped, grey cotton jacket. Brown hair peeking out from a black baseball cap with a bright red flash on the brow. High cheekbones, smooth skin, dark eyes.

He picked up a chip from the plate Sully had pushed in front of him and nibbled it tentatively. And smiled.

"Cheeps," he said again.

"There you go," said Sully. "You're welcome. You speak English?"

The guy ate another chip, and then – quicker – several more, one after the other, but otherwise didn't respond.

"Guess not." Sully fished for his phone, tapped for a bit and said, "Must be Czech? Us, we're *anglitsky*. Is that right? You speak *anglitsky*?"

At the last word, comprehension seemed to dawn, and the guy said a couple of rapid-fire sentences, looking from Sully to Hutch and Jed and back again, evidently waiting for a response.

"Sorry, we don't speak Czech."

The guy looked blank again.

"How about German?" said Hutch. "*Sprechen Sie Deutsch?*"

This brought a look of relief from the guy and another few sentences, this time in German.

"Hutch?"

"I've no idea."

"Thought you could speak German?"

"I can say, 'Can you speak German?' And 'Where is the bus stop?' That's about my lot."

"Well, this is all very jolly," said Sully. "He likes chips, I can tell you that."

"Cheeps," repeated the guy, helping himself to another handful.

"Honestly, between Captain Chip here, and the Pocket Rocket there – " Sully left the sentence unfinished. "All I can say is, this is not the boys' trip I was promised. I could have taken the train to Ayia Napa – "

"You couldn't."

"Nit-picking, Hutch. Mere detail. By rights, we should be drinking fishbowls and meeting un-choosy girls at beach parties. Not on a train eating chips with someone even weirder than Jed, no offence."

"You were having a great time yesterday."

"I was drunk yesterday. Fat chance of that on this train. I thought going interrailing was supposed to be like *American Pie* on the railway. It's more like *The Polar Express*, without even the hot chocolate. Or *Brief Encounter*, minus the cups of tea."

"All right, grandma, *Brief Encounter*? When have you ever seen *Brief Encounter*?"

"I was misled. It was an arthouse screening in the afternoon porn slot. I didn't know it would be about two old duffers at a train station."

"Cheer up, Sully, we'll be in Berlin in a couple of hours. You've always wanted to go there."

"I have heard legendary tales, it's true." Sully warmed to the prospect, and started on a lengthy rundown of the bars and beer-gardens that were in store for them. Apparently, there was an upside-down bar where the furniture was all on the ceiling, and the lighting on the floor, which – rather than a novelty – sounded to Hutch like the head-swirling end-point of every bar crawl he'd ever been on with Sully.

"Cheeps," interrupted the guy. Hutch looked up and saw an empty plate.

"And he's back in the room," said Sully. "Hello, what's this?"

The guy had leaned forward and grasped Hutch's wrist across the table, placing his other hand on top. He paused for a moment, with his eyes closed, and then opened them and looked up into Hutch's eyes.

"Well, this isn't weird at all," said Sully. "Told you, *Brief Encounter*. Don't tell him you've got a speck in your eye, dude'll want to remove it with his handkerchief. And then marry you."

"Darling," said Jed, in an aristocratic drawl, "We'll always have the chips to remind us of our love."

"Shut up," said Hutch, withdrawing his arm awkwardly.

"Greetings," said the guy. "I am Vlak."

Chapter 9

The boys looked at each other and laughed.

"All right, Vlak," said Sully. "You *do* speak English, then?"

"Engleesh. Like cheeps, yes?"

Sully laughed again. "Suppose we do. Though you're no slouch yourself in that department."

"Slouch. Hmm. I am Vlak," he said again. "And you?"

Hutch made the introductions, and the three of them shook Vlak's hand in turn. He held each hand as it was offered to him, lingering just on the awkward side of acceptable, closing and opening his eyes each time.

Jed raised his eyebrows at Sully, and Sully at Hutch. And Hutch thought, with any luck, that was that, because who wanted an excruciating chat in mangled English with a random stranger on a train? Look at your phone, avoid eye contact – basically, do what you did if Jed looked like he wanted to talk to you about yetis.

Sully, though, hadn't got the memo. It was admirable, in a way, how he would talk to anyone in any situation, but he really didn't exercise much quality control.

"Where are you from, Vlak? Germany?" he said

"Ger-many." Vlak rolled the word slowly. He spoke in a soft, measured voice, with only the slightest of accents.

"Is that a yes? Or is he repeating what I'm saying? I can't tell."

"Czech Republic?" said Hutch, pointing out of the window at the countryside. "Czechia. Actually, thinking about it, that's probably Germany out there by now. We've been going for a couple of hours. Are you Czech or German? Sounds like you speak both languages?"

Vlak shook his head, puzzled. "Lang-widge-uz."

"Where. Are. You. From?" said Jed. "Your home?"

"Yes, home," said Vlak, brightening. He raised his finger and pointed out of the window.

"That's Germany, out there, Vlak," said Sully. "Is that where you're from?" And then to the others he said, "Though I've never met a German who can't speak English."

"Home," said Vlak again, and jabbed his finger a little more pointedly.

"North?" said Hutch. "Vlak? What is that name, Scandinavian? Danish or something, is it?"

Vlak smiled agreeably, but didn't reply.

"It was easier when he just ate chips," said Sully. "You knew where you were with Vlak when it was all about the chips."

"I travel," said Vlak, suddenly. "Travel from home," and he pointed up and out of the window again.

"What's further north than Denmark?" said Hutch. "If only we had a couple of college-educated geographers on board. Oh wait, we do."

"Very reductive," said Sully, "thinking that geography is all about countries and maps. A common misapprehension."

"You don't know, do you?"

"Not my area," said Sully, after a slight pause. "More a southern hemisphere specialist myself. Ask me anything about Australia. Not anything, obviously."

"Sweden? Russia? Estonia?" said Jed, hazarding a guess at a mental map of Europe. "They all speak English there, though. Maybe not in Russia. Where's Finland from here?"

"God, you're both hopeless. Don't you ever go to lectures?"

"Lectures?" said Sully. "I am not familiar with this word."

"You are Hutch? You are Sully? You are Jed?" said Vlak, suddenly. "We are English." He beamed at them.

"Well, you're not, mate. You're a mystery. Where are you going, anyway?"

"Train," said Vlak. "I travel."

"You said. Where to?"

If Vlak understood the question, he didn't reply –

he simply looked out of the window again, occasionally glancing back at the others and smiling.

"Fishbowls," said Sully. "Girls. Parties. I'm just saying."

"Be fair," said Hutch. "It's not his fault. You can't speak his language, whatever it is."

"Yeah, he speaks Czech *and* German," said Jed. "More than you can. Vlak's all right, aren't you, Vlak?"

"I am all right, Jed," said Vlak.

"Christ on a bike."

"Yes. Christ on a bike. English," said Vlak. "We are talking English. English talk."

Sully laughed at that. "This has all been most entertaining. But I think I'm going to leave you boys to it. I'm having a snooze. Wake me up when the holiday starts getting good again." He rested his head against the seat-back.

Hutch checked the map on his phone – still an hour and a half to Berlin. And unless they wanted to stand in the corridor, they were stuck at this table until then with the most random person they had met so far.

Hutch nodded at Jed and got up. "Toilet," he said. Anything to break up the journey.

"Toilet," said Vlak, beaming. "Very good. What is toilet? I am still learning English."

"Good luck," said Hutch to Jed. "Don't tell him where we live, that's my advice."

When Hutch returned to his seat, five minutes' later, Jed was on his phone watching a video, with Vlak leaning in to see the screen. Hutch made out a few words – pyramids, star alignment, construction technology – and shook his head. Jed was engrossed in one of his men-in-their-underwear YouTube channels and, for once, had an interested audience.

Hutch opened his own phone and checked his socials, sent a few messages. Sully was snoring beside him. Over on the conspiracist side of the table, they had moved onto the hoax Moon landings, one of Jed's favourite topics.

"This is moon?" said Vlak.

"You know we never went, right?" said Jed. "It was all filmed in a hangar in Utah. You can tell from the photos, the shadows are all wrong."

"U-tah," said Vlak. "Han-ger."

"Why would anyone fake a mission to the Moon?" said Hutch, despite himself, having heard Jed on the subject many times.

"To beat the Russians to it," said Jed, and he would have launched into a further explanation, only he was interrupted.

"And this is spacecraft?" said Vlak. "Interesting. Small."

"Exactly!" said Jed. "It was only a model – Stanley Kubrick had stuff left over from filming *2001*. No one could have flown that to the Moon."

"I agree," said Vlak. "Very dangerous. Not possible."

"God Almighty, the pair of you, as bad as each other."

Sully stirred and stretched. "Are we there yet?"

"But pyra-mids," said Vlak. "The man in the video wrong, Jed."

"Well, would you listen to that," hooted Sully. "Vlak's learned some new words. Have you been reading the dictionary together while I've been asleep? Playing Scrabble?"

"Pyramid a very simple construction," said Vlak. "Aliens didn't build."

Hutch and Sully roared with laughter, pointing delightedly at Jed.

"Even Vlak thinks you're bonkers!"

"Sod off. You believe what you want. I'm saying there's room for doubt, that's all."

"Jed." Vlak was pointing at the next video delivered up by the algorithm. "See, lines in desert."

"The Nazca Lines," said Jed, to more hoots of derision. "In Peru. Huge lines and figures spreading over hundreds of square miles. No one has ever really been able to explain them."

Hutch grabbed the phone to see the video. "Except DaggerOf Truth49.com, obviously. He knows all about them. Good old D.O.T.49, very reliable source, I've no doubt."

"I can explain," said Vlak. "These lines made by aliens for landing craft. I know."

"Ah, Vlak, we were just beginning to like you. Don't encourage him."

Chapter 10

Vlak, it appeared, had the sort of benign tolerance for Jed and his conspiracy theories that Hutch had never been able to muster.

In the flat – on the rare occasions they bumped into each other – Hutch could just about manage to stay amused for whatever Jed was worked up about on that particular day. Atlantis, Machu Picchu, engineered viruses, The Illuminati, fluoride in the drinking water, Area 51, ghost stations on the London Tube housing missile silos – you name it, Jed had an opinion and a video to back it up.

He'd pretty much gone through his full repertoire, as far as Hutch could hear, and to be fair to Vlak, he was still watching and listening. Hutch would have pretended to be asleep ages ago.

Vlak did laugh at some of the videos – quite loudly – which wasn't exactly the response Jed was looking for, but maybe it was the language barrier? At one point,

Hutch could hear Vlak repeating, "Flat? Earth? Disc?" as if he was unfamiliar with the words.

Anyway, he kept Jed occupied, and that had to be a good thing.

An hour from Berlin, Hutch noticed a conductor enter the carriage and start working her way down, checking tickets and passes.

He nudged Sully and got Jed's attention, and then scrolled through his apps to open his train pass.

"Tickets," he said, when he saw Vlak looking at him.

"Tickets, Hutch. Yes."

Jed closed down his video and looked for his own train pass, and then brought up the day's ticket, before placing his phone down on the table.

Vlak peered at the screen. "Tickets for travel," he said. "Interesting."

"Interrail," said Jed. "Mobile train pass, on the phone. I'd rather have had the paper one – less chance of being traced."

"Here he goes again. Who'd want to trace you, the pocket police?"

"You already told the Mystery-Soc nerds where you were going," said Sully. "MI6 would just have to ask them."

"If they could get in to club night – they'd need to know the secret password."

"Good point, Hutch. Though it's the one he uses for everything – OrcLover123."

"You're both very funny."

"I need ticket," said Vlak, suddenly.

"Good luck with that," said Hutch. "I don't think they like it much if you get on without a ticket."

Vlak pulled his sleeve up to reveal a smartwatch with a larger-than-usual black screen – rectangular, with a row of tiny buttons and indentations. He touched a button and put his arm on the table next to Jed's phone. His smartwatch blinked.

"I have ticket. So I have good luck." He smiled at Hutch.

The conductor reached their table and spent a minute or so checking everyone's passes. When it was Vlak's turn, he leaned forward and touched her arm lightly, while presenting the small screen on his wrist. It shimmered briefly – almost like a 3D effect. The conductor stared at the screen for a second, then nodded and thanked him in German. Vlak replied, also in German, and she moved on to the next row of seats.

"Touchy-feely kinda guy, aren't you, Vlak?"

"Touch-feel, yes. It is useful. I like connection," he said.

"Don't we all, Vlak?" said Sully. "Where do you stand on fishbowls and parties?"

"Ignore him," said Hutch. "That watch, though?"

"Watch," said Vlak.

"Your smartwatch." Hutch gestured at Vlak's wrist. "Pretty cool. I haven't seen one like that before. What is it?"

"Like a – phone?" Vlak pointed at Jed's, still on the table. "But on my arm."

"I know what a smartwatch is, mate. I mean, what make?"

"Make?"

"Brand? Is it an Apple Watch? One of the new ones?"

"Not new," said Vlak. "Old. Not latest version." He pulled his sleeve back down, over the watch, hiding it from view.

"If you say so." Hutch shrugged.

Part of the fun of Interrail – belting around Europe on trains, going wherever you wanted – was that you got to meet all sorts of interesting people. The website said so. No, the website *promised*.

And if Hutch's Insta was any guide, everyone else's summer rail trips seemed to involve legendary benders with Australian backpackers, and hook-ups with preposterously attractive people on hideaway Croatian beaches. Whereas they had the Hobbit Pocket Master in tow, and the only other traveller they had really talked to in over two weeks had the conversational skills of Jar Jar Binks. Maybe they should have gone to Ayia Napa after all?

Hutch checked the map on his phone again. Coming into Berlin, finally.

On the one hand, knowing Sully, the drinking would be starting up again very soon. But, look on the bright side, they would be saying farewell to Vlak, who was definitely not going to be featuring in any train-buddy selfie. The guy was just plain weird – and that was saying something, given that they were travelling with a man with a *bratwurst* in his pocket.

The train slowed and pulled into the station, and passengers started to get their things together. Hutch and Sully grabbed their backpacks from the overhead racks; Jed did his usual pat-down to make sure nothing had escaped his pockets during the journey. He retrieved the sausage and munched on that in the meantime, as they all stood in line in the carriage, and then made their way out onto the platform.

"Right then, Vlak," said Sully, while Hutch craned his head looking for the exit sign. "It's been – I don't know what it's been. Entertaining? But we're heading off. Berlin awaits."

"Ber-lin," said Vlak. "What is Ber-lin?" He looked around, quizzically, along the length of the train and then across to the pillars, gantries and ascending escalators.

"This is, you dolt," said Sully. He pointed at the sign on one of the platform columns. "Berlin Hauptbahnhof. Main station. End of the line. Nice to meet you and all that, but we have beers to drink in an upside-down bar."

"No," said Vlak.

"Say again?"

"They said I must take the train. This is train."

"What are you talking about?" said Hutch.

"To go home, I need to take the train."

"Right, good for you. Good luck."

Vlak looked again at the train they had got off, and appeared confused.

"But Sully says this is – Berlin?"

Sully rolled his eyes, and caught Hutch's attention – made a 'Let's get moving' signal with his hand. Hutch nodded and pointed towards the exit.

"Yeah, Berlin," said Jed. "Why, where did you think you were going?"

"The train." Vlak gestured at the carriages behind him. "They said, the train to Ath-ens."

"Athens?" said Jed. "You mean in Greece?"

"You think this is Athens?" Sully shook his head, wonderingly.

"Jesus," said Hutch. "The man's worse at geography than you lot. Two countries beginning with G and he's come to the wrong one."

Chapter 11

Voice recording, Plzeň site, Czech Republic:

X-Team agent
- Sorry to interrupt, Prof, but you're going to want to hear this.

Head of Operations, BEVI Research Unit
[response unavailable]

- We're getting there. Should have it on the low-loader within the hour. But listen, there's something else, before we start shifting it out of here. The craft still has some residual power.

[response unavailable]

- No idea. Half of what looks like a propulsion unit fell off in the forest somewhere – we're still gathering up the bits. The cabin hardware could be fuelled by space dust for all I know. But I pressed a big green button on the console –

[response unavailable]

- Yeah, well I didn't think of that, obviously, or I wouldn't have done it. Anyway, it didn't self-destruct, but what looks like a navigation panel lit up. Located further down the cabin, away from the bio-tank. There's a sort of flight-deck area. The panel has screen overlays, and you can swipe through various file hierarchies.

[response unavailable]

- Yes, apparently they can swipe, manipulate a screen. They've got fingers, limbs, anyway, at a guess.

[response unavailable]

- Sod off. Tentacles?

[response unavailable]

- Very funny. Do you want to know what I've found or not?

[response unavailable]

The Wrong Stop

- Looks like Matey accessed some local mapping before he legged it. Tentacled it. And by local, I mean Earth. There's an open schematic that shows the location of the craft – here in the Czech Republic – and then there's a long, straight, dotted line that leads to a mystery destination. Have a guess.

[response unavailable]

- You're no fun. Greece, of all places. Athens in particular. I reckon that's where Matey's heading.

[response unavailable]

- Your guess is as good as mine. But it's the best lead we've got. I'll get the craft back to you asap, and you can get the pointy heads – no offence – to dig into it a bit more. For now, I've got the boys and girls checking all roads and transport heading in the direction of Greece – which from here, I can tell you, is a lot of bloody directions, so I'm going to need more people on this.

[response unavailable]

- Really? Whatever we want? Chief must be hot for Matey? Tell him we're on it – and that we'll discuss bonuses later.

―――

Urgent communication (Level: Classified)
To: Director (Europe), Bureau of External Visitor Incursions (BEVI)
From: Professor James Storm, Head of Operations, BEVI Research Unit (Germany)

'Chief – the latest information [*link* to extract from X-Team read-out] suggests a plausible scenario. Greece and Athens. But there are significant unknowns – not least, the asset's status or capabilities. And while we have a possible destination, we have no idea why the asset might be heading there.

There are also conflicting reports from agents on the ground in Plzeň and Prague – due, in part, to the limited information that we have felt able to release, even to the X-Team.

I'll be blunt – no one knows what they are looking for. Humanoid is the best guess, from an initial look at the craft's internal layout and dimensions. We should know more once we get it back to the research unit.

In the meantime, we're following up potential sightings heading east to Prague, south to Vienna and north to Berlin – though, given the latest information regarding Athens, Berlin seems unlikely.

Anyway, I hope you meant 'full funding and resources' because given the amount of ground the team has to cover, this is about to get expensive. Once you ask ground operatives to look out for an alien, they start seeing them everywhere.'

Chapter 12

"Athens," repeated Vlak. "The train goes to Athens, they said."

Sully shrugged. "You're in Berlin, mate. I don't know what to tell you. Wrong way entirely. You got on the wrong train."

"Wrong train," said Vlak. "There is other train. To Athens. Yes, I see."

Hutch picked up on that. "Wait. You didn't think it would just be one train, all the way?"

"Yes," said Vlak. "Train to Athens. They – "

"We know, they said. But you can't get to Athens on one train. You have to change trains. Loads of times, probably."

"Change trains." Vlak nodded his head slightly. As if he was only now beginning to get to grips with the concept of trans-European train travel.

"God, how did you get this far?" said Sully. "You're

as bad as Jed, he'd probably be in Lisbon or somewhere if it wasn't for us."

"Says the man who thinks you can get to Cyprus on the train."

Then something else occurred to Sully, as all four of them stood there on the platform. "Don't you have any luggage?"

Vlak looked bemused – or more bemused, it was difficult to tell, given his general air of detachment.

"Bag? Backpack?" Sully pointed at their own gear, resting at their feet.

"Possessions," said Vlak. "No, I don't have. I lost when I – arrived." Then he smiled. "I have pocket, like Jed." Vlak pulled at his jacket to show an outside pocket. "But empty."

"I mean, seriously, this guy – " Hutch gave a short, incredulous laugh.

Jed reached down to one of his thigh pockets and pulled out a folded map with a red cover. He rolled Hutch's backpack onto its side and spread the map out. "Look," he said, pointing, "this is a rail map of Europe. We're here, in Berlin."

"Berlin," repeated Vlak, though with nothing that sounded like recognition.

"Exactly. And you need to go here, to Greece."

"Greece."

"You know, Greece, the country?"

"Kebabs. Retsina," said Sully, helpfully. "Erm, Mamma Mia, is that Greece?"

"Jesus," said Hutch. "Heathen. Athens, the Parthenon, the Acropolis."

"Acropolis," said Vlak. "Yes, I must go there. Acropolis, in Athens."

"Right," said Jed. "Now we're getting somewhere."

He traced the route on the map with his finger, watched closely by Vlak.

"You've already come the wrong way. Should have gone south to Vienna from Prague, then to Budapest, then – let's see – " Jed peered at the lines on the map, "Bucharest, then Sofia. That's Bulgaria. Then I think you have to take a bus to Thessaloniki, and then, yes, you can jump on the train again all the way to Athens from there."

"Athens. The Acropolis. Good," said Vlak.

"But you've come north instead, to Berlin, see? You'll have to go to Vienna first from here, and it's going to take days, mate. You need to change trains, at all those stations. Change, got it?" Jed mimed getting off and getting back on again with his fingers.

"Change trains. To Athens. Yes."

"You just use your rail pass. Like before?" said Jed, pointing at Vlak's smartwatch.

"Right then," said Hutch. "Are we good to go?" He gave Jed his map back and righted the backpack.

"We can't just leave him," said Jed. "Look at him."

Vlak was still staring intently at the sign that said 'Berlin,' as if there was some further mystery to be solved. Or as if it might suddenly change to 'Athens' if he stared hard enough. He didn't seem particularly concerned by anything Jed had told him, but that was fairly concerning in its own way.

"Well, we're not going to Greece," said Hutch.

"Kebabs and retsina, to be fair," said Sully. "Maybe Vlak's on to something. Anyway, isn't Cyprus near Greece?" Sully still seemed to nurture a distant hope that Ayia Napa wasn't out of the question.

"Let's get him on his first train, at least," said Jed. "Won't feel so bad then, abandoning him. You'll be all right once you're on the train, won't you, mate?"

Vlak smiled. "All right, mate, yes."

Hutch sighed, got his phone out, and ran a search. He wasn't quite sure how Vlak had become their problem – though the beauty of putting him on a train heading far away from Berlin meant he'd soon be on some other sap's to-do list.

"Berlin to Vienna? The next one's the night train, departs 18.52, gets in at seven tomorrow morning. How about that?"

"Brilliant," said Jed. "There you go, Vlak. You've got about three hours to wait, then you can get the night train to Vienna. OK?"

"OK, Jed. Vienna, Budapest, Bucharest, Sofia, Thessaloniki, Athens," said Vlak. "I remember. Change, change, change, change, change. Then Acropolis."

"I'd say he's got it," said Hutch, feeling a little better about cutting him loose. Maybe it was just the language thing? He did seem to know what he was doing now, anyway.

"Seems very – complicated," said Vlak. "Why not one train? Get there quicker."

Sully shook his head in wonder, wide-eyed. "Have you ever *been* on a train before, Vlak? Seriously?"

"Yes. Yesterday. Yesterday, first time. Today, second time."

"Christ – and you picked Athens for your first trip? From where, Estonia?"

"Esto-nia," said Vlak.

"You're a brave man, I'll give you that," said Sully. "Jed isn't allowed to go to the shops on his own. Look, tell you what – "

"No," said Hutch. He knew what was coming.

The thing about Sully that endeared him to most of the people he met was that he liked everyone, or at least took everyone at face value.

Sure, he took the piss out of people, but he took the piss out of everyone – piss was extracted on an equal opportunity basis, as far as Sully was concerned. He was everyone's friend, and a gatherer of waifs and strays – in college, at lectures, in pubs, at parties. Jed's very presence on this trip was evidence of Sully's good nature, and here he was, about to scoop up another oddball.

"Oh, come on," said Sully. "We can't leave him in the station on his own for the next three hours. He could end up anywhere."

"He just needs some help," said Jed. "Backpacker code."

"Pocket-packer."

"Sod off. Anyway, we're kind of responsible for him now."

"How do you make that out? We just happened to sit next to him, because there was nowhere else to sit."

"That's the point of interrailing, isn't it? Go new places. Meet interesting new people."

"Interesting is one word for him."

"And we can give him some kit. Come on, he's lost all his stuff. Spare toothbrush at least, I've got one somewhere."

"Course you have. Why don't you give him your gimp-suit while you're at it?"

"You're being very mean, Hutch. It's the decent thing to do," said Sully. "I mean, look at him. If little Jed here was all alone at Tallin station – "

"Geography finally coming back to you?"

"His little pockets all empty, wouldn't you want to think that some kind strangers would help him out?"

"Yeah, come on, Hutch. It's only a couple of hours."

"That's settled then," said Sully. "Hey, Vlak, what do you say? How about you hang out with us until your train goes?"

Chapter 13

The boys had planned to spend one night in Berlin – or 'One Night, Ten Bars,' as Sully had badged it. Originally, Hutch had wanted to stay longer, maybe book a hostel for two or three nights and see the city properly.

The issue, as always, was managing Sully's expectations. "Hostel?" he had said. "Dude, the clubs don't close until eight am, what do we need a hostel for?"

Hutch put his foot down about the hostel, but in the end had agreed to just one night in the city. It was probably for the best. Sully couldn't kill them all in one night, surely?

Consequently, they were booked onto the night train to Brussels the following evening, for the final leg of the journey home, giving them – "Approximately thirty-one hours of dedicated Berlin bar time," said Sully, looking at his phone. "We can spare a couple to help Vlak out, surely? The Vlak-Meister. The Vlakster. You're going to hang with us for a while, Vlak, OK?"

"I will hang," said Vlak.

"A word?" said Hutch, gesturing along the platform. They moved away from their packs and left Jed with Vlak. He had found a spare toothbrush, still in its packet, and had offered it to Vlak, who held it in front of him like it was a stick.

"Something wrong?"

"You tell me. You don't think any of this is weird? That he's weird?"

"He's interesting, your word, I'll give you that."

"He didn't speak any English when we first sat down. You don't remember that? Fluent Czech and German, no English. And now he's chatting away, look." Hutch pointed over to where Jed and Vlak were deep in conversation.

"Fast learner. They're all like that in Scandinavia."

"Estonia. Baltics."

"Wherever. They all speak it better than us. Maybe he was just rusty?"

"He hasn't got any luggage. Says he lost his bag. He's never been on a train before. He thought he was in Athens. Shall I go on?"

"What's your point? Seems harmless enough."

"He's just weird, is all. And now we're stuck with him for a few more hours."

"If weird is your benchmark for who we hang out with, I draw your attention to Exhibit A," said Sully, nodding.

Along the platform, Jed was excavating his pockets

and laying out more items on top of the backpacks. He seemed to be looking for something, and then called out in triumph, brandishing a telescopic selfie stick. Jed fixed his phone into the mount, as Vlak looked on impassively, and then raised the stick and three-sixtied his way around, finishing up standing next to Vlak with his thumbs up. Jed, at least, seemed to be enjoying Vlak's company.

"Fair enough," said Hutch. "But we stick him on the night train and that's that, OK?"

"Think of the story we can tell. The rugby boys might have the fishbowls and the girls, but we met Forrest Gump on a train from Prague."

They sidled back to where Jed was busy repacking – re-pocketing – and Hutch scanned the platform for the exit. "Escalators that way," he said.

"Hang on, I need the toilet again," said Sully.

"Toilet?" said Vlak.

"That word's got to be the same?" said Sully. "Toilette? Toiletten? You know … ?" And he dropped his hand and gestured, as if spraying a short, but unruly, hosepipe.

"Ah, toilet," said Vlak. "I have heard. Yes. Evacuation of the bladder. Interesting."

"If you say so," said Hutch, laughing – mouthing 'Weird' to Sully over Vlak's shoulder.

Sully strode off in the direction of the toilets and, after a minute or two, Hutch followed him, leaving Jed and Vlak with the bags. Inside, Sully was already ensconced in a cubicle if the groaning noises were any guide.

"All right, Sully?"

"Full evacuation in progress. Bear with."

"Something you ate?"

"I hope so. Otherwise I've just discovered a new parasitic species."

Hutch finished up and left him to it, and when he got back outside, Jed and Vlak had moved closer up the platform with the bags.

"He may be some time," said Hutch.

"Scott of the Cramptarctic?" said Jed. "Ernest Crapleton?"

"Very good. Yes, Captain Oates is suffering badly from the polar winds."

"Ah, indeed, the Roaring Forties. Always dangerous."

They stood idly for another minute, at which point Vlak said, "I will visit Sully's toilet. Jed, will you visit the toilet?"

"No, you're all right, mate. You go. Try not to breathe in."

Five minutes later Hutch looked up from his phone. "What *are* they doing in there?"

"Sully? Could be a while yet, you know what he's like. Vlak, no idea. Evacuating his large Estonian bladder."

"Honestly, we've been in Berlin almost an hour, we're still on the bloody platform."

Hutch walked back into the toilet to see what was happening, and encountered Sully emerging from the cubicle. "At last, thought you'd fallen in – "

He stopped in mid-sentence and stared, as did Sully.

Vlak was standing by the row of sinks, chopping one hand back and forth under the tap. The sensor kept triggering the water, and then cutting out again, missing Vlak's hand every time. He was staring at the tap intently, as though it was a game he hadn't quite mastered.

Hutch and Sully also noticed something else. Vlak had unzipped his jacket to reveal a grey-green T-shirt, and had taken his baseball cap off and put it on a side shelf.

Having given up with the tap, Vlak was now looking into the mirror above the sinks – looking closely at his almond-shaped eyes, and running his fingers down his cheeks. He touched his shoulders, where wavy brown hair now fell, freed from his cap. Touched both sides of his nose, and then looked down at his T-shirt and back up again.

Vlak saw Hutch and Sully behind him in the mirror, smiled and then turned to face them properly.

They looked at each other, before looking back at Vlak. The hair, the face – the contours under the T-shirt.

"Hello," she said.

"But you're – "

"I am Vlak, yes. It's very interesting. I'm ready now."

And she zipped up her jacket, tucked up her hair and put the cap back on, and turned to walk out of the toilet, leaving the two boys open-mouthed.

Chapter 14

Traffic news, website of the Allgemeiner Deutscher Automobil-Club (ADAC – General German Automobile Club):

'Heavy, slow-moving traffic on Bundesautobahn 6, between the Czech border and Nuremberg, is expected to continue for the next two to three hours.

Regional police report that the delays are being caused by the assisted transportation of hazardous waste material, and the tailback currently stands at eight kilometres.

All vehicles are advised to avoid Bundesautobahn 6 until the police-led convoy has cleared the highway. Diversions are in place, and drivers should follow the posted signs.

This page will refresh automatically with any new updates.'

Email to: Mr Jed Turner
From: Admissions, Student Services
cc: Personal Tutor, Department of Geography
Subject: Failed assessment, interruption of studies

'Dear Mr Turner,

Further to our previous correspondence, to which I have had no reply, I am afraid that your place on the undergraduate programme in the Department of Geography has now been suspended.

As you know, from earlier conversations, you have not met the requirements of the course for some considerable time. I am informed that your attendance at workshops, seminars and tutorials has not improved, despite previous warnings.

You have been offered every assistance by departmental staff but have chosen not to engage with the process. In addition, the academic assessment arranged for you remains incomplete.

After discussion with your tutors, we have taken the decision to withdraw you from the second year of your degree course.

This is classed as an 'interruption of studies,' although recommencement within the degree programme is not guaranteed. I strongly urge you to reach out to your Personal Tutor if you wish to continue your studies at this university.'

Chapter 15

Jed blew his lips out, and put his phone back in his pocket. The email wasn't much of a surprise. He'd known it was coming.

Maybe more of a surprise was the relief he felt. He was sick of pretending that it was going to be all right, and now it definitely wasn't going to be all right, he felt lighter somehow.

It was a shame the trip was almost over. The trip he hadn't planned on – the one Sully had had to talk him into at first. The one he hadn't been certain he would enjoy, because he didn't know either Sully or Hutch that well, despite living in the same flat for a year. Plus, he didn't usually like to be out of his room for that long.

But actually, it had been all right. And now it turned out that the train trip across Europe and back was all that he had. It wasn't like there was anything else to get back for now.

Vlak was still squatting on the ground a few feet away. He'd come out of the toilet and had asked Jed for the map again, and now had it spread out on the floor. Upside down, realised Jed, as he watched Vlak trace a slender finger in a roundabout route from Berlin towards Athens.

Hutch and Sully came out of the toilet together a minute or so later, took one look at Vlak and beckoned Jed a few paces away.

"There's been a development," said Sully.

"Sorry to hear it," said Jed. "Dodgy sausage?"

"Not me. Him." Sully jabbed a thumb towards Vlak. "Or rather – "

"Her," said Hutch. "Turns out, Vlak's a girl. Dude's not a dude."

"Bollocks."

"Definite absence of those," said Sully. "I'm guessing," he added, hastily. "We didn't see."

"What are you talking about?"

"Look," Hutch said, pointing. "Closely."

All three of them turned to stare at Vlak, still engrossed in the map. Hutch and Sully knew what they had seen, and now that they knew, it seemed obvious. There could be no mistake.

"She took the cap off, unzipped the jacket. We saw her hair and face properly. And, you know – " Sully made a rolling motion with his hands at chest height. "Definitely not a dude."

Jed cocked his head slightly and squinted. "I guess. Could be."

"Are you mad? Have you ever seen a girl? Look at her!"

"I knew there was something off about him. Her," said Hutch. "We should just get rid of her. Too weird. Agreed?"

"Let's not be hasty," said Sully. "When does a hot girl ever want to hang out with us? A hot Scandinavian girl?"

"Estonian."

"Whatever."

"In fact, when do any girls want to hang out with us?"

"I hang out with girls," said Jed.

"Yeah, your mum," said Hutch, automatically.

"Hilarious. Josie, actually, in – "

"Sasquatch girl doesn't count, either."

"So, what's the rush?" said Sully. "It's not like anything's changed. It still doesn't seem right, abandoning them. And it's not like she lied or anything. Just kept her cap on and her jacket zipped up. It's not her fault Jed's blind."

"You didn't know either!"

"And you don't think she's strange, in any way? At all?" said Hutch.

"She's kooky. When you're a hot girl, you're kooky. It's in all the movies. Kirsten Thingy. Zooey Whatsername."

"What's the harm?" said Jed. "I think she's all right, anyway. I like her."

"You would, lizard boy."

They stood there for a moment, at an impasse, until Vlak suddenly folded the map up and got to her feet.

"Are we going to hang out, then?" she said, offering the map back to Jed. "Until 18.52, yes, Hutch? Then I take the night train. Vienna. Not Berlin."

Sully brightened and clapped Hutch on the shoulder. "Course we are. Hutch here is just planning our next move. We've got plenty of time, so what's it to be?"

Hutch looked dubious – there was definitely something off about this, but nothing he could put his finger on. If it was a scam – if Vlak was some kind of con artist – Hutch thought it would have played out by now. But she hadn't yet asked them for money or stolen anyone's –

Hutch checked his bag. OK, good. Passport, still where it should be.

She hadn't asked them for anything, really. But there was no denying, it was off.

Sully and Jed were waiting for him to speak. What the hell, thought Hutch, they'd be rid of her by seven, either way.

"Well, we said we'd do the Berlin Wall first thing."

"You said."

"Berlin Wall," said Vlak. "You want to go and see a wall in Berlin?"

"Ha! Yes, exactly, Vlak, thank you," said Sully. "No, we don't. Pub?"

"Pub," agreed Jed.

Sully led them out of the main station, down to the

river and along the embankment to the Zollpackhof, a riverside tavern.

This was the other thing about Sully, the so-called geography student – a passing acquaintance with urban and cultural geography, a woeful ignorance of spatial data science, yet an encyclopaedic knowledge of Europe's finest bars and beer gardens.

He had at least twenty places in Berlin pinned to his phone map, but anticipating that Hutch might attempt to steer them into a museum or gallery at any minute, he had clearly picked the closest to the station. Ten minutes later, they were sitting on a riverside terrace under shady trees, and even Hutch was forced to admit that this didn't seem like the worst idea Sully had had on the trip.

The nibbly-foot fish spa in Zürich, that had been the worst idea he had had. Sometimes, late at night, Hutch could still feel the tingling in his toes.

"Traditional Bavarian food, anyone?" said Jed, once they'd ordered four beers from a passing waiter. He brandished a menu.

"Which is?"

"Let's see. Pork knuckle, no. Bavarian radish, God, no. Liver dumpling soup, jeez. Ah, sausages. Excellent. And chips."

"I like chips," said Vlak, gazing out over the water beyond. "And I like the pub. A very good place to hang out."

She took her baseball cap off, hair falling around her shoulders, and lifted her face to the sun. "Not so much like home," she said. "Warmer here. I like that, too."

Jed glanced at her – unobtrusively, he hoped – as she basked in the sun. He looked back at Hutch and Sully and nodded. OK, definitely a girl. Odd. Kooky, even. But a girl, for sure. And one who seemed to want to hang out with them, at least for an hour or two. What, indeed, was the harm?

Jed stared a bit more intently, though Vlak didn't seem to notice the attention. If you stared this much at Sasquatch Josie, she stared back and asked if you wanted a photo.

The waiter arrived with their beers, and they sat for a moment admiring the glow of the afternoon sun through the glasses. Sully, Hutch and Jed reached for a beer, clinked cheers and drank.

"That's yours," said Sully, indicating the fourth beer.

"Mine," said Vlak. She looked confused.

"Don't worry about it, drinks are on us."

Hutch raised his eyebrows at that. He might have known Sully would be out to impress. Maybe this was the scam? If it was, she was putting in a lot of hours – and putting up with an increasingly animated Jed – for a free beer or two. Good luck to her, if that was the extent of her long game.

Sully pointed at the beer and made a drinking gesture with his hands. "It's good," he said. "German – cars and beers, you can't go wrong."

Vlak leaned forward and sniffed the beer. Sully

picked up his own drink again and took a sip. "Don't you drink beer?" he said. "Honestly, I think you'll like it, but if you don't I'll get you something else."

Vlak picked up the glass, put it to her lips and tilted it. Drank.

And then dropped the glass – the beer spilling everywhere – as she slumped forward, her head lolling, before coming to rest with one cheek firmly on the table.

Chapter 16

"Vlak?" Sully touched the girl's shoulder, but she was unresponsive, flat out on the table.

"What's wrong with her?"

Hutch looked around the beer garden. A few other late-afternoon drinkers were sitting at distant tables, enjoying the sun and a pint. No one had noticed.

"Vlak?" Sully shook her shoulder this time, and Vlak stirred, half-smiled and then slumped to the table again. She breathed loudly out of her open mouth, snoring slightly.

"Well, this is absolutely fantastic," said Hutch. "Couldn't be better. Told you she was a liability. Now what?"

"She looks out of it," said Jed. "Completely pissed."

"She can't be! She had one sip."

"Fuck's sake, Vlak!" Sully shook her again, and Vlak wafted a hand at him and groaned.

"This isn't good," said Jed.

"You think so, genius?"

"No, I mean, it looks like Sully roofied her."

"Christ."

"I only bought her a beer!"

Hutch looked round again. A waiter appeared from the far side of the beer garden and walked past with an empty tray, casting a curious glance at their table. Hutch moved instinctively closer to Vlak and put an arm around her shoulder in what he hoped looked like the act of a concerned friend.

"Now what?"

"Try and sober her up?"

"She can't possibly be drunk!"

"Maybe she had a bad reaction, I don't know."

"Fuck's sake."

"So you keep saying. This is your fault," said Hutch. "Hang out with a kooky hot girl, you said. What's the harm, you said?"

"How was I to know she was allergic to beer?"

"We should have just left her at the station. Told you it was all a bit weird."

"So *you* keep saying." Sully shot back a glance at Hutch. "Not helping."

"What time is it?" said Jed.

"About half-five."

"She'd need to be back at the station in an hour, if she's going to catch her train."

Hutch thought about it for a second or two, saw a glimpse of light, and then said, reluctantly, "We can't put her on the train like this."

Vlak stirred again, said something unintelligible, and put her cheek back on the table, mouth open to the sky.

"Unbelievable," said Sully.

"You're the one that roofied her."

"Sod off."

"She'll have to come with us," said Jed. "Take her to the hostel, she can sleep it off there. She's going to miss tonight's train now anyway. She'll be fine by tomorrow."

Both Hutch and Sully looked at Jed, shaking their heads in disbelief.

"Are you mad?"

"Well, we can't leave her here."

"We can! We could call someone. Hospital. Police, I don't know."

"You want to spend the next few hours explaining how a girl in our company, that we don't know, has accidentally become so drunk or drugged she can't walk after one sip of beer?"

"When you put it like that – no, not really."

Hutch considered the alternative. It was only marginally more attractive an idea, but it was entirely in keeping with this shitshow of a day so far.

"Take her to the hostel? And how's that going to look? Three blokes carrying a drunk girl up to their room? None of this looks good."

"Maybe she'll sober up a bit on the way?" Jed got his phone out and tapped on the map. "Hostel's the other side of the station, a fifteen-minute walk from here."

"Or maybe," said Sully, "she's not a drunk girl at all. She's a drunk bloke. Put her cap back on, sort her hair, help her into the room. I mean, it's not like *we* knew she was a girl, and she's not going to speak to anyone else in this state. As far as the hostel will be concerned, Vlak here is just another casualty of an afternoon well spent in Berlin. They'll have seen a drunk backpacker before."

Hutch didn't want to admit it, but this also wasn't the worst idea Sully had had on the trip.

"That could work," said Jed.

"We'll check ourselves in," said Sully, "and then sneak her in, put her in one of the beds."

"And we cut her loose first thing tomorrow?" said Hutch. "Agreed? When she sobers up. She's on her own after that, I don't care what you say. This is way too stressful."

Sully went off to pay for the beers, while Hutch and Jed got Vlak to her feet. She mumbled a bit, but was able to stand, and Hutch placed the baseball cap back on her head, tucked her hair in, and zipped up her jacket.

There – just your regular, very good-looking, very pissed bloke being carried by his mates. And definitely not a very hot, very weird girl about to be sneaked by strangers into a backpackers' hostel.

Hutch and Sully put on their packs and took it in turns to support Vlak under one arm as they walked slowly back along the river embankment towards the station.

Jed stayed out in front, plotting the route on his phone. He led them back around the station and up a block or two, before turning along the edge of a park to find the hostel entrance. Hutch and Sully took a breather against the wall outside, backpacks at their feet, with Vlak propped up between them.

Jed disappeared inside and came back five minutes later with a key card.

"Room with four beds," he said. "They need to see your passports, I told them you were on your way."

"Don't tell me this is actually working?"

"We've still got to get her past reception, but it's pretty busy in there. I don't think it's going to be a problem."

Hutch and Sully nipped inside, leaving Vlak with Jed, and checked themselves in, too. Then all three regrouped outside.

"Ready? Let's go. And just keep moving."

Jed pushed the doors open and they moved through as a group, partially obscuring Vlak as they passed the reception desk. It was as Jed had said – plenty of other backpackers milling around, between lounge on one side and luggage storage area on the other. No one noticed four more arrivals, and they punched the button on the elevator and rode up to the third floor.

"Thank Christ for that." Sully breathed a huge sigh of relief once the room door had closed behind them.

They dropped their packs and laid Vlak down carefully on one of the lower bunks. Her head sank into the pillow, and they arranged her vaguely into a recovery position and stood back.

Her eyes were closed again now and after a few more seconds she seemed to fall into a deep sleep. Her heavy breathing sounded above the traffic noise from the street below. Hutch reached down and took her cap off – that one simple action revealing the truth of the matter.

They'd just successfully sneaked a very hot, very unconscious, very kooky girl into their dorm.

"I feel like I'm in an Eighties' gross-out movie," said Hutch. "*Animal House* or something. I mean, my dad used to watch those. I can't believe anyone ever found this sort of thing entertaining. I think I'm going to have a heart attack."

"Six o' clock," said Sully, looking at his phone, not one for introspection. "Pub?"

"Hell, yes," said Hutch. Sully's ideas had been looking up all day. This was the best yet.

"What if she wakes up?"

"No chance of that, look at her."

They closed the door quietly behind them and followed Sully out of the hostel – already bringing up his Berlin bar list on his phone.

They came back sometime after midnight, shushing each other as they crashed into the room, giggling. To be fair, they'd made a fine attempt at Sully's list – not quite ten bars, but definitely seven, maybe eight. One had had circus rides and Jed had been a bit sick in a carousel. Kebabs had been involved at some point. Basically, a great night, and a big tick for Berlin.

A faint glow lit the room – from the streetlights outside, or passing cars. Enough anyway to pull their clothes off without putting on a light.

There were twin beds on one side of the room, but Hutch had drawn the short straw and got the top bunk above Vlak, which he grumbled about as he considered the stepladder. He could hear the other two still giggling on the other side of the room as they got into their beds.

Hutch put one foot on the bottom rung and let it take his weight. It creaked. He swung upwards, peering down between the rungs – there was almost a shimmer around Vlak, still out for the count on the bed below.

On the bed? Above the bed? The glow seemed to reach under Vlak's body, as though she was suspended a few inches above the mattress.

Hutch shook his head and belched. His stomach lurched a little, and he hauled himself onto the top bunk and lay there, eyes closed, head swimming, beer fumes rising.

Bloody Sully.

Chapter 17

Urgent communication (Level: Classified)
To: Director (Europe), Bureau of External Visitor Incursions (BEVI)
From: Professor James Storm, Head of Operations, BEVI Research Unit (Germany)

'Chief – the craft arrived safe and sound, under wraps, though local authorities are still twitchy, thinking we were shifting hazmat. You might want to have another word, make the news go away.

Anyway, it's in the bunker and I've authorised access for essential personnel only – Level 3 and higher.

You really have to see it! Power source, navigation, life support – it's like nothing we've ever seen before.

Main initial takeaway – extrapolating from things like apparent cryo-tank tech, seat pitch, nav controls – is that Matey is definitely humanoid, normal proportions. Basically, two arms, two legs and a head – about five foot ten tall, going from the cryo-tank dimensions.

There's some residual operating power, so we're pulling what info we can from any files that we can access. I've got the Xeno guys on it and as soon as we get anything else useful, we'll forward to agents in the field. That should help with the search.

Talking of which – the X-Team have trawled CCTV at all exit points in Plzeň and Prague, and questioned local staff on the ground. After running biometric and ID checks to exclude normal traffic, there is one potential lead – but it hardly fits with the findings from the craft's nav unit, which is that Matey is heading for Athens.

[*Image attached, partially obscured*] There is no match or record for this individual, but note that the direction of travel is Berlin, ie, north and not south. Still awaiting confirmation from CCTV at all stations en route to, and including, Berlin Hauptbahnhof.

I'll put my guys on it, just in case, but I think it's a red herring. Best guess for finding Matey is still any route south to Greece.'

Voice recording, Prague, Czech Republic:

X-Team agent
- Berlin doesn't make any sense, boss. Matey's going to

Athens, according to the info from the craft. I've already got people here and in Vienna, checking road and rail – those are the obvious routes.

Head of Operations, BEVI Research Unit
[response unavailable]

- Mine not to reason why, I know. And you think this image could be them? It?

[response unavailable]

- Looks like a kid in a jacket and baseball cap to me. You think they arrived with a suitcase full of clothes from Urban Outfitters?

[response unavailable]

- Disguise capabilities? I guess so. But if I have to stop and search every kid in a baseball cap between here and Berlin, Matey's going to be long gone. Plus, I'll probably get arrested.

[response unavailable]

- I don't know, I was hoping the cryo-tank might have had a few more clues in it. You've had it for hours now. Nothing sloshing about in the bottom, to give us an idea what we're dealing with?

[response unavailable]

- Tentacles wasn't amusing before. Saying gills doesn't make it funnier.

[response unavailable]

- I thought we were supposed to be the planet's leading ET research unit? Seems like we don't know anything about our guy or what he can do? Even though we've got his vehicle? I mean, if the Martians had my car, they'd be able to tell what sandwich I had for lunch. Probably be able to figure out my DNA from the bits of cucumber on the floor.

[response unavailable]

- Humanoid's not much help when I'm scanning a zillion actual humans.

[response unavailable]

- Suppose. It's frustrating, though. I almost wish he did have green skin and tentacles, we'd have caught him hours ago. People tend to notice things like that. Who's going to think there's anything odd about a kid in a baseball cap?

[response unavailable]

- All right, I'll look into it myself. Prague's a bust in any case. If he was here, he's gone now. Don't worry, if he's sightseeing in Berlin, we'll find him. We'll put out a fake APB, get the local cops and public to help us narrow down the search.

Chapter 18

Hutch groaned and clasped his head. Light flooded in through the window – no one had remembered to pull the blinds when they had got in late last night.

He checked his phone. Eight am. Great, he had been hoping it was more like eleven – he never could stay asleep after a night's drinking. His stomach fluttered, churned and growled, like a flatulent hamster was trying to make a nest inside him.

Sully and Jed were snoring away. Even Vlak was still asleep below him. She *had* to be feeling better, after – what? – fourteen hours in bed.

He pulled on some clothes, grabbed the key card and let himself out of the room. Coffee, downstairs, might help.

He found the café attached to the hostel, grabbed an outdoor seat, gulped down an enormous Americano, and ate a blueberry muffin.

Better.

A police siren started up in the distance and then got louder as two unmarked cars raced past, engines gunning as they slowed and then accelerated around the corner beyond.

Hutch winced at the piercing sound. He squinted at the morning sun and blew his cheeks out. Was there anything worse than a hangover on a hot, sunny day? Shower next, then a proper breakfast. That should sort him out.

He bought four takeaway coffees, stuck them in a cardboard holder, and carried them up to the room. Sully and Jed hadn't moved, but Vlak was sitting on her bed, feet on the floor, and smiled as he came in.

"You're up," said Hutch. "How do you feel?"

She looked about her, as if searching for the right answer.

"Different," she said, finally. And then, "Interesting."

That's about how Hutch felt, too, if by 'different' and 'interesting' she meant 'a bit crap'. "Coffee?" he said.

She looked at the proffered cup. "No," she said. "I think I mustn't drink."

"Fair enough." Hutch still felt a bit dicky himself. Be all right after some more food. He put the other cups down by Sully and Jed and poked them awake, to their obvious annoyance.

And then he remembered the train – Vlak's train, the one she should have taken last night.

"Sorry, you missed your train," he said. "We

thought we better bring you here. We didn't know what else to do. You were – out of it."

"Out of it," repeated Vlak. "The drink. Of course."

"What *was* that?" said Hutch. "I mean, you barely had a sip. Are you not supposed to drink, or something? If it affects you like that?"

"I think I shouldn't drink. Yes."

"You *think*?" Hutch shook his head. Not any less weird today, then. Anyway, not their problem anymore. They had one day left in Berlin before their night train to Brussels, and Hutch was not going to spend it babysitting a strange girl who collapsed after a mouthful of alcohol.

Sully was up, doing something unspeakable in the bathroom, if the noises were any guide. And Jed was attempting to rehouse himself inside his travel shorts, which always took some time, given the amount of flapping and clanking it entailed. Vlak looked on, seemingly unconcerned, as Jed exposed various bits of flesh while bending, stretching and strapping things together.

He turned round, finally, red with the exertion, and sat down to pull his trainers on.

"Vlak's feeling better," said Hutch. "She'll be fine to get her train," he added pointedly.

"Thank Christ for that. Thought you were a goner."

"Goner, Jed?"

"Lightweight, more like," said Sully, emerging from the bathroom. "Thought Estonians could drink? Never seen anyone do that before. Even Hutch here can manage a couple of shandies before he keels over."

"Bog off, I kept up with you, didn't I?"

"All right, Russell Crowe, calm down."

"How are you not feeling like crap, Sully?"

"It's all in the genes, boss. Plus – " and Sully pointed at the bathroom – "it's better out than in. I'd give it a minute if I were you."

"Jesus, Sully!"

"The pleasure is all mine. Right, who's for breakfast?"

Sully grabbed his shoes and put them on, and stood there waiting while Jed patted his pockets down one last time.

"Coming?" he said to Vlak, who was still sitting on the bed. She'd put her baseball cap on and had tucked her hair back under it again. "Food?"

"Chips?" she said. "Can we have chips?"

"You don't muck around, do you? Hardcore. Chips for breakfast. I dunno, you might have to have – what was it, Jed? Bavarian radish?"

"Don't, you're making me feel queasy."

"The café's got fried eggs," said Hutch. "*Spiegelei*. I remembered a German word. Bagels, too. And other stuff."

"Don't suppose the bar's open?" said Sully.

"You're an animal. Breakfast first. Then let's figure out what we're going to do today – you know, when we've said goodbye to Vlak." Hutch spelled it out pointedly, so there was no misunderstanding.

He knew only too well what Sully was like – if they weren't careful, he'd be inviting Vlak to come and stay with them in London. They'd endured Sully's cousin on their sofa for a week once, and as Sully's cousin got up at six every morning to Joe Wicks himself awake and then drink all the milk, that had been a very long seven days.

They trooped out and made their way down to the self-service café, where Hutch found them an inside table. He needed a Full German before he felt he could tackle sunlight again. Or loud noises.

He and Sully lined up at the counter, leaving Jed and Vlak at the table, and they worked their way along, picking up food as they went.

"Suppose we're buying hers?" said Hutch. "I don't think she's offered to pay once."

"You look like she does, you don't need to buy anything yourself. I don't mind, anyway. It's been – different, I suppose, is the word."

"That's what she says. What the hell. Get her breakfast and then we're done. And we don't talk to anyone else, at all, for the rest of this trip. Promise?"

"Whatever. They don't have chips. I'm getting her Doritos, two packs. She looks like a Doritos kinda girl."

"If she wasn't so self-evidently bonkers, Sully, I'd say that she'd be a perfect match for you. Apart from the drinking capacity."

"I could soon train her up, mate, don't you worry." Sully looked at Hutch and laughed. "Oh relax. Breakfast and gone, promise."

They shared the food out at the table and sat there for a while, eating in silence. Sully had opened a pack of Doritos, and Vlak was picking at them tentatively – "Like chips?" she'd asked, and Hutch chalked up yet another oddity. Not that he'd ever been to Estonia. Who knew what chemically processed snacks were available there?

People came and went past them, and the café filled up as it approached a time of the morning more attuned to hungover backpackers. A large TV on the wall blared as a member of staff switched it on and then turned down the sound.

Jed tilted his head and downed the last of his bottle of energy drink. Between the fried eggs and the high-fructose sugars, he was feeling infinitely better, thank you very much. Ready for whatever the day had to offer, provided it wasn't straight back to the pub.

Despite what Sully and Vlak had said, Jed actually quite wanted to see the Berlin Wall. One of the murals supposedly contained clues to the whereabouts of a hidden cache of Nazi gold, though as the source was an engineering student in Mystery-Soc with an unhealthy interest in the Third Reich, Jed wasn't fully convinced. Still, it was something to do before the inevitable trip to the pub.

The TV caught his eye. He watched as a news bulletin unfolded – no sound, but German text ticker-taping along the bottom of the screen. Nothing he could understand.

The pictures flicked from a line of police cars

outside a railway station to some grainy CCTV footage of a person jumping onto a train as it started to pull out. The footage paused, and then zoomed in on the still picture – even grainier – and Jed looked hard at it.

Then turned to Vlak, who was speaking to Sully, and plucked at her arm.

"Vlak. Vlak," he said, more urgently, as she turned.

"Yes, Jed."

He pointed up at the TV screen.

"That person there, in the picture. That's you, isn't it?"

Chapter 19

DW News broadcast, Deutsche Welle international news channel: [Running caption – "Police hunt dangerous fugitive."]

'A manhunt is underway across Germany for a fugitive that Federal Police sources are describing as "extremely dangerous."

His identity has not been released, but he is believed to have entered Germany from the Czech Republic and has known connections in Athens, Greece. The authorities remain tight-lipped about the reason for their extensive search, citing national security concerns, while the heavy police presence at major transport termini across Germany suggests the highest level of alert.

Police have released this CCTV footage, showing an individual of interest boarding a Berlin-bound train at Prague's main station yesterday.

A Federal Police spokesperson told us: "We are

extremely anxious to locate this individual, who may have travelled recently to Berlin on the EuroCity train from Prague via Dresden. If you have seen this person, or have any information, please contact the police immediately.

Under no circumstances should you approach this person, who is considered armed and highly dangerous."

This appears to be a fast-moving investigation. Terrorist connections cannot be ruled out, although no specific threats are known. Meanwhile, the public is urged to remain vigilant.'

Chapter 20

Hutch and Sully turned in their seats to see what Jed was pointing at.

With the TV sound off, the background noise in the café was a low chatter from other people, the occasional clink of cutlery and crockery, and the hiss from the coffee machine.

The still from the CCTV stayed on the screen a few moments longer. A zoomed-in shot from on high of a slender person in a zipped-up jacket, face largely obscured by a dark baseball cap with a distinctive flash. Could be almost anyone, if you hadn't already spent several hours sitting next to them on a train and then carrying them unconscious across Berlin – in which case, it was unmistakably Vlak.

The CCTV picture disappeared, to be replaced by video of police patrolling a railway station, before cutting back to the newsreader, who started on the next story.

Sully turned back and dropped down to the table on his elbows.

"That was you? No way."

"That *is* you!" said Hutch, joining him, looking across at a wide-eyed Jed, who dropped down, too, leaving a curious, upright Vlak, until Jed signalled her down, frantically.

Hunched down, they all looked at each other across the table.

"What the – "

"Yes," said Hutch. "Exactly. What. The. – "

"Why are you on the telly?" interrupted Jed.

"Telly?" repeated Vlak.

"TV. Television. Why are you on the television, like a wanted person, with police and everything?"

"They want to catch me, I think," said Vlak.

"No shit!"

"Yes shit," said Vlak. "They're chasing me, I suppose."

"You suppose!"

Sully shushed them and looked around the café – everyone else just eating, drinking and chatting, and not hanging out with someone suspicious off the telly. In fact, all four of them now looked highly suspect, crouched down around the table and whispering furiously. He gestured for them all to sit upright again and, as an afterthought, leaned forward and grabbed the cap off Vlak's head. She shook her hair free.

"No one's noticed," he said. "But in case they put that picture up again … "

"Why are they after you?" said Hutch. "What have you done?"

"I haven't done anything," said Vlak. "I just want to go home."

"You must have done something! You're on bloody German *Crimewatch*."

"Dangerous fugitive," said Jed, reading from his phone.

"What!"

"I've found a news report, shoved the headlines into Google Translate. Vlak, it says here that you're very dangerous."

The three of them looked at the admittedly odd, but entirely unthreatening girl, who had been eating Doritos with them a few minutes earlier.

"What's she done?"

"Can't tell. Doesn't really say. Though I think this sentence says 'terrorist'."

"Fuck's sake!"

"I haven't done anything," repeated Vlak. "This is not true, what they are saying."

"They don't chase you, and put you on TV, and call you a terrorist, if you haven't done anything."

"If she is a terrorist," said Sully, "she's a fairly useless one. No offence. Only thing she's done so far is knock herself out."

"I am not a terror-ist," said Vlak, stumbling over the word. "But they do want to catch me. This is clever of them, I think."

Hutch had had enough. If they had been in a bad

situation yesterday, this was much worse. They wouldn't just be explaining to the local police how they'd managed to unwittingly drug a complete stranger and hide her in their room. They'd be sitting handcuffed in a basement under an interrogation light while burly men in shades shouted searching questions about harbouring a wanted terrorist. Questions for which there were currently no good answers.

"I think you should leave," he said to Vlak. "Don't care what you've done." He turned to the others. "Right now, we can still say we didn't see the reports. No one else has noticed her. She can just disappear. We don't need to get involved."

Sully looked unconvinced. "This holiday is finally getting more interesting and you want to call time on it?"

Even Jed weighed in against him. "Yeah, don't you want to know what she's done?"

"I have not done anything, Jed."

"So you keep saying. They must be after you for some reason?"

"Yes, I think so." Vlak touched her hair and then one cheek, and hesitated. It was difficult to know if that was an admission or a mere acknowledgement.

A loud siren sounded outside as a car flashed past, followed by a speeding police van. Everyone flinched, and they all rose from the table in unison.

"To the room?" said Sully, to nods of agreement. And then to Vlak, urgently, "Don't put your cap back on."

They walked in twos to the elevator in reception, and then rode to the third floor.

"I must take the train now," said Vlak. "To Vienna, and then Athens. Like Jed said."

"It doesn't go until seven tonight," said Jed. "There might be a day train, I suppose."

"What's in Athens, Vlak?" said Hutch. "Why there?"

"It's – complicated," said Vlak. She seemed unwilling to explain further.

"You don't say."

"I do say, Hutch, yes. Complicated."

"We should get out, too, guys," said Jed. "If they think she's in Berlin, it's not going to take them long to trace her here."

"You're talking like you still want to help her!" said Hutch. "Did you not hear the words 'dangerous terrorist'?"

"She says she isn't," said Jed. "You heard her."

"That's like lesson number one at Terrorist Training Camp! They probably teach you that the first day. 'Look harmless, say you're not a terrorist, hoodwink some multi-pocketed twit.'"

"Well, I believe her," said Jed, once they were back in the room. "I'll come to the station with you, Vlak, check if there's an earlier train."

"Thank you, Jed."

"Me, too," said Sully. "This is more like it. The rugger boys have *no* idea where all the action is this summer."

He threw his belongings together and stuffed them in his backpack. Jed was already at the door, waiting with Vlak.

"Coming?"

"God, I suppose so." Hutch packed quickly and hoisted his pack onto his shoulder. His hangover, he realised, was long gone, battered into submission by the cortisol currently careering through his bloodstream. "This is a terrible idea," he said. "I just want that on record."

Coming out of the elevator into the downstairs lobby, they unconsciously split into twos again – Jed with Vlak, out in front, Hutch and Sully bringing up the rear. Outside and further down the street they turned for the main road and the station, still in their pairs.

Either something had changed, or – given the circumstances – they were simply hyper-sensitive to their surroundings. In any case, it seemed to Hutch that everyone was watching them as they got closer to the station. And it certainly wasn't his imagination that there were more police cars and security vehicles arrowing in on their destination. The passing sirens gave them a jolt every time.

With flashing blue lights ahead of them in the distance, Sully called a halt. "This isn't going to work," he said. "It's blocked off ahead. Let's get out of here."

Jed had his phone open. "Back the way we came and into the park opposite the hostel. We can regroup there."

They turned together, but Sully held firm for a moment.

"They think she's a bloke wearing a cap, right? And the cap's off." He looked at Vlak. "Trust me, you don't look like a bloke. But take your jacket off, too."

He gestured at Vlak, and then helped her off with her jacket and stuffed it in his backpack.

"There." He looked at her approvingly. "Right, final touch. Hutch, put your arm round the girl and let's go. Jed, where's this park?"

Chapter 21

They found a grassy spot deep in the park, under a tree and away from the main paths.

"No surveillance cameras here," said Jed, looking around. "Should be safe for a while." He lowered himself to the ground gingerly – he'd been known to topple over from a badly weighted pocket before now.

"All right, James Bond."

"Double oh bell-end."

"The Man with the Golden Pocket."

Sully lay back on the grass, breathing heavily but laughing. "I'm knackered. This pack weighs a ton. I'd have brought less stuff if I'd have known we were going to be running away from the police on holiday. I feel you should have mentioned this, Hutch, in your little spreadsheet."

Hutch waved a hand, dismissively, too out of breath to talk, and rested against his own backpack. Jed spread his arms behind him, palms out, supporting himself.

Vlak completed the circle, sitting cross-legged with her arms folded in front of her.

Just four regular backpackers, taking in the morning sun in a Berlin park.

"Right then," said Hutch. "Don't you think it's time you told us what's going on? We've made ourselves accomplices now. You kind of owe us an explanation."

"It's complicated," said Vlak.

Sully snorted. "Yeah, you said. But you're going to have to do better than that. Little Jed here can't go to prison, look at that face."

"No one's going to prison," said Hutch, though he wished he sounded more confident about that.

"You reckon?" Sully shook his head. "I don't see how this ends well. You saw the TV. They're after her, and we helped her."

There was a silence, broken by Hutch, who looked at Vlak and said, "So?"

"I'm hungry," she said. "I need to eat. Then I'll tell you."

"To be fair, I could do with something, too," said Jed. "I'm starving."

"You just had breakfast!"

"And then I ran across Berlin. My breakfast calories have long since been used up."

"Chips," said Vlak.

"With the chips again! Where are we going to get chips, in a park?"

"From that *bratwurst* van, over there." Jed pointed at a parked vehicle a few hundred yards away, with an open hatch and a few plastic tables and seats. "I saw it when we came in."

"Don't you still have your emergency sausage from the train?" said Sully.

"Very funny. No, I ate it."

"Jesus, guys!" Hutch raised his voice. "Are we seriously talking about chips, when – you know?" and he pointed at Vlak.

"What's the harm," said Sully. "Get her some chips, hear her story."

"I feel like you've said 'What's the harm' a few times now. And each time, there has been, oh I don't know, a shitload of actual harm. In case you've forgotten, we've recently done a runner with a dangerous fugitive terrorist."

"Well, I'm getting chips," said Jed. "Just in case we do have to run again. Four lots, right?"

He came back five minutes later with four plastic trays and shared them out, and Vlak wasted no time in diving in. They gave her a few more minutes while she ate, and then looked at her expectantly once she had tucked away the last chip in the tray.

"It's true, they are looking for me," she said. "I expected it."

"Why, though? What have you done?"

"I told you, I haven't done anything. I just want to go home. But I thought it would be easier than this. I thought I would get on the train and go to Athens – to the Acropolis."

If anyone noticed that Vlak's diction had improved

again, they didn't say. Whatever slight accent she had had, had also disappeared.

"So, you haven't – I don't know – murdered anyone? Or blown anything up?"

"I have done neither of those things, Sully."

"Then you've got nothing to worry about. It must be a mistake. You could hand yourself in, clear it up."

Vlak looked him in the face, held his gaze. "Sully, if they catch me, they will do bad things to me."

"What does *that* mean?" said Hutch. "Who's 'they?'"

"Bet she escaped from a facility," said Jed. "They've got these secret bases where they run medical tests and stuff on people. You know, like poor people, homeless people – they promise them money and then lock them away underground, expose them to experimental drugs and viruses. I saw it on – "

"Do not say YouTube," said Hutch. "Absolute bollocks."

"Yes, bollocks," said Vlak. "I am not homeless, Jed. I have a home. I'm trying to go back there. But I got on the wrong train by mistake. And now they are chasing me, and if they catch me, I am afraid of what they will do to me."

"Seriously? This makes no sense at all," said Hutch. "Does anyone else think this is absolute nonsense?"

"It's true, Hutch, I promise."

"You keep saying you want to go home? But you're heading for Athens? And you come from Estonia? They're in opposite directions, for God's sake."

"I don't come from Estonia, Hutch. I don't know where that is."

"You said you did!"

"I did not." Vlak sighed, and said, "It's – "

"And don't say complicated. We know. We're sitting in a park, on the run from the police because it's complicated. If you don't come from Estonia, where *do* you come from?"

Vlak sighed again. "I didn't want to tell you. To tell anyone. Because it might be dangerous for you to know."

"Bit too late for that. And what do you mean, dangerous?"

"I said she'd escaped from somewhere!"

"No, Jed. I only want to go home," and Vlak pointed a tentative finger upwards.

"Not Estonia then? What's north of Estonia?"

"Russia?"

Vlak shook her head slowly, and jabbed her finger higher.

"Christ knows, then. Wait a minute, Svalbard, is that a place? Polar bears and stuff. Oh, and secret research stations, I bet that's it!"

"It's easier if I show you," said Vlak. "Just a moment."

She held her left wrist out in front of her, displaying her large, rectangular smartwatch, and tapped a couple of tiny, indented buttons in sequence.

The deep, black screen blinked twice and then two shallow edges rose from the shorter sides of the watch.

There was another flicker and a 3D hologram image emerged from the screen and rested upon the raised sides, before expanding and tilting in a lateral orientation.

"What the ... "

Vlak leaned across with her other hand and pinched and expanded the hologram image, which now hovered a few centimetres above her wrist. Faint lines ran between a jumble of dots, and as she separated her thumb and forefinger once more, the dots grew larger and resolved themselves into small, filled circles.

She zoomed in further on one of the circles, which showed an elliptical line stretching from either side, around a larger, brighter ring. There was a small caption next to the circle – not letters, but an arrangement of shapes and lines that resembled hieroglyphs.

Vlak looked up into astonished faces.

"There," she said, pointing her finger into the hologram at the planet. "Home."

Chapter 22

Urgent communication (Level: Classified)
To: Professor James Storm, Head of Operations, BEVI Research Unit (Germany)
From: Director (Europe), Bureau of External Visitor Incursions (BEVI)

'Be advised, chatter from on high suggests that our friends in Washington have got wind of Matey. They intend to acquire and do not intend to share. Special Alien Operations' agents from US black sites in [redacted] are apparently in play and on the ground.

I've had a quiet word with the capital letters at MI6, and the MoD, but they're strictly hands-off when it comes to Anglo-American-ET business. They'd rather we dealt with it and didn't tell them anything about it – they prefer plausible deniability, when it comes to our work. Officially, as you know, we don't exist, so we're on our own with this.'

[*Voice note attached*]:

'Jim – the Yanks don't ever play nice when it comes to things like this. If Matey ends up in Area 51, that's the last we'll ever see of him, apart from an occasional courtesy visit. You certainly won't get to have a cosy chat about interstellar travel with him, so authorise your agents to use all necessary resources to find our little pal, pronto. Let's get him bagged and delivered as soon as possible, before the Americans get anywhere near him.

At least we've got the craft now. How's that going? I hope you deep-cleaned the crash site – I don't want so much as a speck of space dust left in Plzeň for anyone to find.'

Chapter 23

"What's that?" said Hutch slowly.

"Where I live," said Vlak.

"Not that, that!" He pointed at the smartwatch, with the expanded hologram still hovering above.

"It doesn't have a name you'd understand," she said. "It is my – help."

"No way," said Jed.

"Fuck. Me." said Sully, extending his hand towards the hologram. His finger shimmered as it broke the boundary, and he grinned. Then laughed out loud.

"You're an alien?" said Jed, with wonder in his voice. "An actual alien?"

"Well, that's bollocks," said Hutch. "Obviously. It's just a – I don't know what it is. Some kind of 3D superwatch thing. Let me have a look, take it off."

"I can't, Hutch, not here, anyway. I'm sorry. It's – connected to me."

"Convenient. And also bollocks."

Vlak touched one of the indented buttons on the screen and the hologram disappeared. The two short, raised sides receded flush into the surface, leaving only the dark rectangle laid along Vlak's wrist. No watch strap or other fastening, Hutch noticed, for the first time.

A minute ago, he had been convinced that this was Vlak's scam, finally playing out. But if that was the case, even Hutch was beginning to question where exactly this went. How did you go from showing your marks a fancy wrist-pod to relieving them of their money, their passports, and the contents of whatever you fancied from Jed's pockets?

"I mean, come on," he said, less convincingly. "You're saying that little circle was an alien planet?"

"Not so little," said Vlak. "And not alien. My home. Where I live."

"I knew it!" said Jed.

"You did not! You only just figured out she's a girl. And now we're supposed to believe she's an alien?"

"It all makes sense. Why they're after her, everything."

"It doesn't make any sense. Aliens, please. Yesterday, it was all Bigfoot and cosmic pyramid builders. You'd believe anything. Sully, help me out here?"

"It does kind of make sense."

"Not you, too!"

"You said it yourself, she's not exactly normal.

Sorry." Sully looked apologetically at Vlak, who simply sat there, seemingly unconcerned by the discussion going on around her.

"You're not buying this, surely? I mean, Jed. Yes, obviously, right up his street. If she said she was Santa, he'd believe it." Hutch suddenly looked like a spark had gone off in his head. "And she already knows what he's like! Sat next to him yesterday, saw his videos. She knew he'd fall for this."

"Maybe, but I'm asking myself a simple question," said Sully. "What's most likely? That Vlak here is an alien? Or that a hot girl – sorry, but you are – has wanted to hang out with the three of us for the last day?"

"I vote alien," said Jed.

"Me, too," said Vlak. "Although, of course, you're really the aliens, as far as I'm concerned."

"Well, you're just hilarious," said Hutch, though he did concede that Sully might have the slimmest sliver of a point. They'd spent two and a half weeks up until now on trains and in hostels in some of Europe's most alluring cities, attracting precisely zero female attention. Much like the last year in college, too. Vlak might not be normal, but neither was her continued presence in their company.

"Sully, what is a hot girl?" said Vlak. "I do not understand the context."

Sully looked embarrassed. "You know, hot. Fit. Gorgeous. Erm ... a beautiful face and erm ... all that," he tailed off.

"Interesting," said Vlak. "Are humans not all hot, then? It is surely simply a varying arrangement of standard chemical elements within a breathable skin? You all appear the same to me."

"Jed? Hot? Oh, dearie me, no. That's not how it works on Earth at all."

"Are you all kidding me?" Hutch raised his voice. "She's on the run" – pointing at Vlak – "we all just helped her, so we're seriously in trouble, and we're sitting around discussing whether or not she's an alien?"

"Let's say she is …" said Sully.

"I am," said Vlak.

"Prove it then," said Hutch.

"Did you not see the Obi-Wan shit? From her wrist-thing?"

"Not that, something else. That could just be some new gadget from China or something." He turned to Vlak. "I can't believe I'm saying this, but if you're an alien, what are you doing here? Why have you come?"

"I was on my way home – to where I showed you. There was a malfunction in the drive system. My ship crashed on your planet."

"Your ship. Yeah, right. But you managed to get on a train, with your alien ticket, and learn to speak, what, three languages, with your alien decoder thing? Because you need to get to Athens, that well-known hub of alien activity? Have I missed anything out?"

"You seem agitated, Hutch. I don't understand what is difficult about any of those things?"

"You don't? Hilarious. English, by the way, very good. Couldn't 'speak a word' when we first met you – " Hutch did air quotes – "and listen to you now!"

He got up and stomped around under the tree for a bit. The more he thought it through, the more preposterous it seemed. And meanwhile, they were sitting here in a park with a wanted fugitive.

"It was difficult to understand at first," said Vlak.

"Sure."

"Why you speak in more than one fashion," she said. "You share the same planet, yet the manner of speaking is very different, even within a short distance. It takes my help – " – she indicated the smartwatch – "some time to calibrate."

"Is that right?" Hutch said, loaded with sarcasm.

"Yes, Hutch. Once I touch an individual, I am able to analyse their core neural networks. The help builds a communication bridge, which improves the longer I'm in contact. It's very simple."

"Amazing." Jed had leaned in, hanging on every word.

"Amazing bollocks, more like."

"I like this word," said Vlak. "Most euphonious. We do not have an exact equivalent, although from the context, I assume that you do not believe me?"

"None of this is proof! You were on a train with a rail pass and ticket! We saw you show them to the conductor. You eat chips, for God's sake!"

"The amylose starch products containing ascorbic

acid and potassium? The micronutrients align well with my metabolism. They are surprisingly nutritious."

"She's good, I'll give you that." Hutch shook his head. "All right, explain the train."

"I scanned available transport on arrival. You have aircraft, it seems, but they are extremely rudimentary and rely on the flight of a pressurised cabin propelled by a kerosene-based fuel, which is manifestly dangerous. Your fixed-rail transport system, while more indirect, is less risky."

"And the pass, the ticket that you showed?"

"I told you, I can access the neural networks of those I am in close contact with. It is a straightforward matter to make individuals of your species 'see' what it is they want to see."

"Are you listening to all this? Sully? Come on!"

"I genuinely don't know. But this is very entertaining. Who cares if she's an alien or not?"

"The police, presumably? Or have you forgotten about them?"

"Yeah, good point. I had actually. Now what?"

"Hutch." Vlak got to her feet and stood in front of him. "I understand that you are finding this difficult to believe. Please, let me show you."

Vlak reached out. Startled, Hutch made as if to pull away, but her fingers closed around one of his wrists, and she held his gaze.

There was something, thought Hutch – maybe nothing. The tiniest of flashes, sparks, in his mind. A roll of the stomach. A blink as he tried to clear his head.

Vlak held onto his wrist for a moment longer, then released him.

"Bunny," she said. "It's all right, Neil will stop them."

Chapter 24

"I told you," said Sully. He stood over the bigger boy, one foot either side, wiry fists still clenched.

The chunky Year 5 kid – loudmouth, ringleader – lay on the deck in the playground, pawing at a fresh scratch on his cheek. He looked faintly stunned. He hadn't seen the punch coming – neither had Hutch, to be fair. Hutch had just wanted to get away from the taunts, but Sully had had other ideas.

Some of the other kids had noticed and were beginning to congregate around them. Hutch heard a chant of "Fight! Fight!" but it had barely been a fight, and it was all over by now.

Sully knelt beside the kid and leaned in, face to face. "He's my friend. I told you not to call him that."

"It's only a joke," the kid whimpered. "Bunny. Like a rabbit. Hutch. Hutchinson."

"It's not funny. And I already told you that, too. If

you or any of your stupid mates call him that again, I'll hit you again. Got it?"

Sully looked him in the eye and saw acceptance, defeat, humiliation. There was no way back for a Year 5 kid, decked by a Year 4 in front of everyone.

Then Sully got back up and was walking away with Hutch, arm around his shoulders, when the teachers finally arrived.

Letter to: Mr and Mrs Sullivan:
From: Gladstone Road Junior School

'Dear Mr and Mrs Sullivan,

Following an incident in the playground today, I am afraid that we will have to ask you to keep Neil at home tomorrow.

We cannot tolerate fighting at school, or bullying of any kind. While I appreciate that Neil was standing up for his friend, Corey Hutchinson, who I understand has had some issues with the other child concerned, it is simply not acceptable to use violence in this way.

Neil is an extremely able boy and I know that this is uncharacteristic of him. Therefore, his suspension is just for one day – though I would like you both to attend school tomorrow morning with him so that we can discuss this further.

Yours sincerely,

Jennifer Potter (Miss), Form 4B'

Chapter 25

"Bunny?" said Jed.

"Never mind." Hutch looked rattled. He hadn't heard that name in years. He looked at his wrist, then at Vlak. "How did you – ?"

"And who's Neil?"

"Me, you idiot," said Sully. "Keep up."

"Did I know you were called Neil? I don't think I did?"

"They didn't call me Sully at birth, did they? What kind of name would that be? But who wants to be a Neil?"

"Fair point, Sedaka."

"You think Neil's bad, wait till you find out what Hutch is actually called."

"Shut up you two!" Hutch was leaning back against the tree, slightly dazed. He gathered himself and addressed Vlak again. "You did something? Didn't you? I felt it."

She spread her hands. "Yes, Hutch. I am sorry. But I wanted to make you see."

"Jesus. It's true? You're an alien."

He said it matter-of-factly this time. He had felt something – some disturbance, some flash. In his mind. In his head. He wasn't quite sure.

In any case, Vlak had seen something in his past that she couldn't possibly know.

And that meant Vlak was telling the truth. It was a fact. She was an alien.

"Jesus!" he said again, as it hit him. "What are we going to do? They really are after her." Hutch realised that he was now also fully accepting that there was a 'They.' Not the police, not anti-terrorist spooks, but the sort of people Jed believed in.

If anything, that was even more disconcerting. That if an alien landed on Earth, there were people whose job it was to chase them. Probably a whole organisation with a fancy name – payroll, job benefits, expenses, the lot. Secret lair under the Tower of London or something.

Jeez.

"We shouldn't stay in the same place for too long," said Jed. "They'll be running face recognition and checking security footage. We should find a safer location."

"All right, Wanker Tailor Soldier Spy. As of this morning, they still think she's a dude in a cap. And I thought you said the park was safe?"

"Nowhere is safe," said Jed, darkly. "You can get

micro-surveillance bugs on Amazon that you could put inside a flower." He looked around, as if considering for the first time that the herbaceous borders might be festooned with listening devices.

"Sorry about him," said Sully. "You probably wish you'd sat on the train next to some nuclear physicists, or someone with a very particular set of skills. Not sure we're what you need if you're an alien on the run. You could hide in one of Jed's pockets, I suppose."

"I don't know about that," said Hutch. "We're ordinary, normal. They won't be looking for anyone like us. And there are tons of backpackers around. Actually, if you think about it, she blends right in."

"As long as she doesn't do any alien shit in public. You're not going to melt anyone, are you? Use your laser? Or levitate, anything like that?"

"Ohhh … " Hutch just remembered something, and gave out a long gasp. "You did, didn't you? Levitate? I saw you in bed, last night, while you were asleep. You were a few inches off the mattress! I thought I was drunk. Well, I mean, I was drunk, but you know – "

"I was probably in rest mode, yes. My body is still adjusting to your gravity."

"This is insane!" Hutch whooped with laughter, and then stopped suddenly, hand over his mouth. "Right, focus. We should move, Jed's right – which is a phrase I never thought I'd utter. Somewhere a bit less open, while we figure out what to do."

"I must stay hidden," said Vlak. "No one else can know I'm here."

"But Vlak, this is huge," said Jed. "You're an actual alien visitor. Do you know how long we've waited for this? First contact?"

"This is not first contact, Jed. The men in your videos are incorrect about many things, but they have identified some of the earlier visits to your planet."

"Told you!" Jed crowed at Hutch and Sully, triumphant to be at least partly vindicated. "So, why not announce yourself? I know they wouldn't have understood in ancient Egypt or whatever, but it would change everything now, if people knew that there really was extra-terrestrial life out there. And your technology must be far more advanced – the things you could teach us … "

"Very perceptive, Jed. You're right, of course. But your species is still in its infancy and seems to mistrust – strangers, visitors, foreigners. If they catch me, I'm worried that they will investigate me."

"Investigate?"

"Perhaps it's the wrong word. Probe, I think, is more accurate?" And Vlak corkscrewed her forefinger into the air. "With instruments," she clarified. "Up the – "

"To be fair," said Jed. "Any time one of us is taken by aliens, there does seem to be a lot of probing involved. There's a fella on YouTube says he's been done a dozen times. Sits on a big cushion to make his videos."

"I don't think this can be true, Jed," said Vlak. "The people I have seen in your videos do not seem to be of the highest intellect. What would be the purpose of a more advanced species probing a lesser?"

"She's got you there, mate. They might dissect you, I suppose, to see where evolution went wrong. Otherwise, I reckon you're safe."

"Whereas your scientists – even with their limited understanding – would be able to determine a great deal by judicious use of the probe. The knowledge would be dangerous in their hands. I can't allow myself to be captured."

"Jesus, no one is getting probed!"

"Let us hope not, Hutch. I believe it to be a most unpleasant procedure, if the gentleman on the cushion is to be believed."

"What about your ship, though? You crashed, right? Won't they have found that by now?"

Vlak punched another set of commands on her alien smartwatch and examined an indecipherable read-out. "Yes. It appears to have been moved."

"Alien-hunter bunker," said Jed, nodding knowledgeably. "Knew it."

"Aren't they going to be able to find out all sorts of stuff from that?"

"There is only a limited amount of information that they will be able to derive from the craft itself. It's imprinted to me. Of course, if they catch me as well – " She left the sentence hanging.

"What are we going to do, then?"

"Well, the train station is out for now," said Sully. "It was getting very blue-lighty there, and we need to come up with a plan. Tell you what – now you won't like it, but hear me out. We should go to the – "

"No chance."

"They're never going to think to look in a pub," said Sully. "Plus, it will be full of other people like us. And it's closer to the station for when we need to get moving."

"Neil makes excellent points," said Jed.

"Bugger off, Jedidiah."

"And it's nearly lunch time, anyway. I'm sure Vlak needs to keep her strength up, don't you?"

"It is imperative, Jed, yes."

"She's not having anything to drink. What happened to you, anyway? Allergic to alcohol?"

"I was not familiar with the compound. It is – alien to me. But a most interesting experience. Out of this world, you might say."

"Alien, out of this world, very good."

"Thank you, Jed."

"God, this is like your dream date. An alien with a sense of humour, and the distinct possibility of a good probing later on."

Chapter 26

They moved through the park looking for a side entrance and then worked their way around the back streets, crossing a couple of major roads to reach the river.

For the purposes of what Jed called 'tradecraft' and the others called 'tossercraft' they kept to the same two-and-two configuration, with Jed and Sully leading twenty yards ahead, checking the junctions. They avoided the blue lights and sirens near the station, and eventually relaxed when they realised that no one was taking any notice of them. Jed seemed slightly disappointed that they hadn't had to take more evasive action.

Back at the Zollpackhof tavern, they took up places at a terrace table with a clear view of the street and handy for the entrance. It was busier than the previous day, and Sully took comfort in the sight of other backpackers, as well as plenty of people in suits or carrying shopping bags. Seemed like his idea might be a good one, after all. Hide here amongst the others, taking time out in a busy Berlin pub.

Jed scoured his phone for the latest news, and turned up a few more hits about the fugitive currently the subject of a massive, nationwide manhunt.

"No mention of anything more specific, yet." Then he saw something else. "Oh," he said, "right, of course, makes total sense."

He turned his phone to show a BBC report about the Plzeň cargo plane-crash site. The agricultural-chemical spillage had been cleaned up, local roads were now open again, and the authorities were reassuring people that there had been no lasting damage to the environment.

"That was you, wasn't it?" He showed Vlak the map location of the crash. "They covered it up! I knew it. Textbook."

Vlak examined the map. "Yes, that's where my craft came down. It was badly damaged and won't fly again. They have it now, though."

"The UFO?" said Hutch. "Those lights in the sky the other night, in the Pils place?"

"We prefer the term UAP, I told you."

"Jed here says you're an Unidentified Aerial Phenomenon. What do you think about that?"

"But I identify as Vlak." She looked puzzled. "Phe-nom-enon? A remarkable thing whose cause or explanation is in question. Yes, that part sounds correct."

"So, what happened? To your ship?"

"Are you familiar with astrodynamics, orbital manoeuvring, and optimal flight trajectories? Or wormhole technology?"

"Space stuff?" said Sully. "God, no. I mean, I've seen *Interstellar*. Didn't understand a word of it."

"Then all you need to know is that something went wrong with my navigation system on my way home, and I crashed on your planet."

"On your way home from where? You mean there are other inhabited planets out there? Three at least, from what you're saying? Our one, yours, and this other one, wherever you'd been?"

Vlak looked confused, and then shook her head sadly. "Three? You really don't understand the universe at all, do you? It is exactly as I learned in my studies. Such an unobservant species."

"You're a student? This just gets better and better." Sully was enjoying himself now. "What do you study?"

"Everything, of course." Vlak looked puzzled again, as if she didn't understand the question.

"Ha! Liberal Arts then. Like Hutch. Bit of everything. Preserve of the perennially indecisive."

"Says the geography genius. One up from sports science, I suppose."

Jed interrupted them and held up his phone again. "Right, here, look. Vienna, I've found an afternoon train. I'll check the connections to Budapest and on towards Athens. Then we just need to get you to the station."

The waiter brought three beers and, when he left,

Jed took out his European rail map and folded it on the table. He began to write train departure times next to the relevant cities for a route to Athens, checking that Vlak could understand.

"A sexagesimal system based on local solar time? Interesting," she said. "Also, confusing."

Sully was busy downing his pint, seemingly fine with the notion that he was sitting in a Berlin pub with an alien. Jed, too – happy as Larry, if Larry was a conspiracy-theory nut whose Christmases had all come at once. Hutch watched him, annotating the map and, bizarrely, pointing out places of interest along the way to Vlak, as if she would have time for a leisurely dip in the thermal baths of Budapest.

"Athens" said Hutch, once he realised the one question they hadn't yet asked. "What's the deal with Athens? Why is it so important for you to get there?"

This was the thing about travelling around Europe with a go-anywhere rail pass. All destinations were possible. If you were in Madrid and said you were off next to Copenhagen, no one would bat an eyelid. Unless you were an alien on the run from a possible probing, in which case travelling by train from Plzeň and Prague via Berlin to Athens just seemed mad. It made no sense at all.

"There is something there I need, in order to return home," said Vlak.

"OK."

"But it's complicated."

"Of course it is."

"I can show you." Vlak proffered her wrist again, but was quickly shut down by Sully.

"Don't do that again! Not here. No alien stuff, remember."

"It's all right, Sully. Give me your device" – she gestured at his phone – "and I can show you."

Vlak placed her arm next to Sully's phone, brought up a slider on her smart-help screen and then flicked. An image flashed across to the phone and Sully turned it to landscape so they could see it better.

It was a photograph of a Greek temple – taken from ground level, from some distance away, with a bright blue sky above soaring marble columns.

The temple stood on the highest part of a hill – the ground fell away sharply to one side – with a visible flight of marble steps in the foreground. A road, paved with broad, dressed stone blocks and lined with large statues and cypress trees, ran up to the temple. A few figures – people – could be seen in the distance.

"Where is that? Athens?" said Hutch.

"Yes. The Acropolis," said Vlak. She touched the photo on Sully's phone and it changed to video, the people in the distance now moving, the scene ahead rising and falling slightly, as if someone was walking while filming.

The temple grew larger as it came into closer view – a rectangle of impressive columns, with a monumental door flanked by high walls, set behind the columns, that blocked any further view inside.

"Parthenon, I guess?" said Hutch.

They all watched as the video played on. The camera panned across the road ahead at one point, taking in some wooden stalls, where people in bright tunics and leather sandals were standing and chatting. The shot lingered on a garishly painted shrine nearby and then swung back, past the outline of a smaller building, to concentrate again on the approach to the temple.

Close to the foot of the marble steps, with the columns towering above, the camera panned upwards, showing the sharp edges of fluted columns. The horizontal slabs and capitals at the top of the columns were decorated with geometric designs in bright red, yellow and blue. Above that, life-sized stone reliefs showed heroic figures in muscular poses, while an even larger assembly of painted sculptures was ranged above within a triangular pediment that ran the width of the building. Right at the roof apex was a golden statue, looking down over the whole site.

"Is this from a movie or something?" said Jed. "One of those old Hollywood things?" He'd started off thinking it was a tourist video, but the temple looked new – in technicolour even – and the people wandering around were all in period dress.

"It is a guide," said Vlak. "To where I need to go. The things I need are in that building."

"What do you mean, a guide?"

"It was provided by the most recent visitor to your planet. It shows the precise location of a transporter device that can be used in an emergency."

The Wrong Stop

Hutch peered closely at the video, now showing an ascent of the steps towards a ten-metre-high door. This was flanked by two armed guards in bronze breastplates, each sporting a wicked-looking spear and a long dagger in a leather sheath. They looked bored. One was scratching his nose, while the other shuffled from foot to foot.

"No way," he said.

"What?" Jed still didn't get it.

"That's – " Hutch could see Vlak nodding. "That's not an old film. That's actual footage. That's ancient sodding Greece."

Chapter 27

Extract from information panel, Acropolis Museum, Athens, Greece:

'Although we think of the building known as the Parthenon as a temple, it almost certainly played a different but significant role in ancient Athens.

It was dedicated to the virgin goddess Athena (*parthenos* means 'virgin') and boasted an enormous golden statue of the goddess (long vanished). But despite its religious dedication, there is no evidence that priests or priestesses conducted ceremonies at the Parthenon, and the building complex did not contain an altar.

Instead, we might view the Parthenon (and other similar ancient Greek 'temples') as a sort of city treasury, housing the collected taxes of Athens, as well as war booty, tributes, offerings, dedications and gifts. Secure internal rooms contained an extraordinary array of valuables – from golden bowls and silver cups to splendid jewellery, ornate furniture, and glittering processional treasures.

Foreign dignitaries and other individuals donated many of the items, which were recorded on stone tablets by the temple's accountants, the Treasurers of Athena.

For reasons of state financial transparency, visitors to the Parthenon were able to view these records, as well as the treasures, though it is not clear how public access was arranged or monitored. It is thought that appointments could be made, and donors were certainly able to enter the inner strongroom to bestow gifts in honour of the city.'

―――

Attachment to video-guide [approximate translation into 'English,' one of the rudimentary communication tools used by inhabitants of Planet 3, Sol System, in the Spiral Galaxy]:

'This information is provided as a public service to travellers. It does not constitute a recommendation or endorsement. Travellers use the information at their own risk.

Visits to this planet are not encouraged. It is a backwater, with little of discernible interest and inhabitants still at Development Stage C. Probing is rife.

A recent visitor – victim of a slingshot trajectory error at the notorious Wormhole Interchange – has provided the following assistance for any future travellers unfortunate enough to land on the planet.

They were able to re-start their craft, and departed without incident, but before they left, they deposited two single-use, field-issue transporter devices [*no exact translation*] in the building shown.

The building lies within the bounds of one of the most advanced societies on the planet [*jocular remark, no exact translation*]. It is surprisingly well constructed, and the vaults are secure and well maintained. It is considered likely that it will remain in use for [*unit of time, no exact translation*].

Travellers wishing to use the devices must first gain access to the building where they are stored – a 'gift' for the 'goddess' will be required [*comment on role of religion in juvenile society, no exact translation*].

Please note, these evacuation devices are for emergency use ONLY – for example, if probing is imminent. Their presence should not be taken as encouragement to visit this planet, which remains undeveloped and dangerous to visitors.'

Chapter 28

Vlak had stopped the video with another tap on the screen. The guards in front of the gilded door froze in mid-movement.

"An emergency guide," she said, "provided by someone from my planet who also landed here."

"Provided by Ridley Scott," said Sully. "Cecil B de Fuck-Off. Come on. That *has* to be from a movie."

Vlak pointed to a set of hieroglyphics in the bottom left of the screen. She tapped her own smart-help and the figures on Sully's phone whirled and resolved themselves into a counter that said '2457.'

"So?"

"Timestamp. That is the number of your years that has elapsed since this guide was prepared."

Hutch did the rough maths. "Four hundred and something BC? Are you serious?" He laughed. "That's actual ancient Greece!"

"Hang on," said Sully. "You said 'recent visitor'?

Two and a half thousand years ago is not what I'd call recent."

"Your notions of time are amusing. So many different ways to measure it, and all of them incorrect."

Jed took a long drink from his beer, put the pint down, and held up a finger to interrupt.

"So, the thing you need to get back home is in the Parthenon? The big temple in Athens on the hill."

"Yeah," said Sully, laughing. "The one your alien mates built."

Jed said "Pyramids" under his breath and soldiered on. "Past those guards, through those doors, inside that building? That's where your device is?"

"Yes, Jed."

Hutch put his own pint down. He suddenly saw where this was going. "Oh, bollocks," he said.

"Bollocks is right," said Jed. He picked up his phone and did a quick search, turned the screen to Vlak. "That's the Parthenon," he said. "Today, anyway."

The familiar, bleached, skeletal outline stood out against a piercing blue sky that showed between the worn columns. Roofless and open to the elements, stripped of its statues and internal walls, it was surrounded by cracked steps and a jumble of masonry, with bare stone and dirt paths to all sides.

"I don't understand," said Vlak. She scrolled the video back on Sully's phone and put the two images side by side.

"It's a ruin," said Jed. "It's famous. You know, like an archaeological site."

"But where is the rest of it? What happened to it?"

"Dunno. It fell down. It's over two thousand years old. That's what happens to stuff."

"And the things inside it?"

"There isn't anything inside it, look. It's open to the sky. You can go and visit it, walk round it. That's what you do in Athens. That's what Hutch would make us do, anyway. Personally, we'd rather go to a *taverna*."

Vlak's shoulders slumped. For the first time she looked worried. Frightened, even. There had been a coolness, a calmness, about her until now. She had shown equanimity, and even amusement, in the face of her predicament, but this seemed to be a blow.

"How is it possible," she said, "that you allow an important building like this to fall?"

Jed was busy Googling. "Earthquakes," he said. "Wars. It got blown up by mistake in 1687. The local people nicked all the stone for building. It's amazing there's anything left at all."

"Bollocks," said Vlak. "Hutch, is that the correct usage?"

"You must have another way to get home?" said Sully. "You being an advanced species and all. A back-up plan?"

"It's complicated," said Vlak. "But, no. This was the back-up plan. My ship was damaged beyond repair. My only hope of evacuation was with the devices on the Acropolis."

Her face, usually impassive, crumpled a little. Hutch tried to comfort her.

"It'll be all right, Vlak. We'll think of something."

"It will not be all right, Hutch. If I can't escape, then I will be probed. Would you like to be probed, Hutch? I can assure you, you would not." She took a deep breath. "Sorry, Hutch. I'm upset. This is all most concerning. I know you live here, but I really wouldn't have chosen to come to this planet."

"Why, what's wrong with it?"

Sully listened for a while to the exchange, which seemed to involve Vlak repeating the words, 'backwater,' 'uninteresting,' and 'dangerously simplistic' quite a lot, and Jed saying, "But what about the Grand Canyon?"

He didn't have anything to contribute himself, but he did think three more beers was probably a good idea. Three and an extra sip in a glass if it didn't look like Vlak was going anywhere for now. It might take her mind off the potential probing and the apparently useless planet she had landed on.

He looked around the beer garden for a waiter. There was one over by the entrance talking to a couple of men, and Sully was just about to raise his arm and catch the waiter's attention when he saw the parked car on the kerb beyond.

There were two other guys in dark suits and wraparound shades standing with their backs to the vehicle. They were clearly with the two blokes now talking to the waiter – similar look – and when one of them leaned forward to talk to the other, his jacket fell open.

Sully was a student. He watched daytime TV,

played GTA, and streamed a load of stuff late at night. He knew a holstered gun when he saw one.

The waiter turned, beckoning the two men into the beer garden. Sure, have a look round, seemed to be the general gist.

"Guys," said Sully, urgently. "Over there." Then, forcefully, "Don't all turn round! Men-in-black, incoming."

Jed sneaked a look. Two blokes straight out of central casting had started to patrol the beer garden, deadpan faces, scanning the tables, eyes invisible behind the shades.

"That's not good," said Hutch. "What'll we do?"

"Don't panic," said Jed. Then, after a pause. "That's all I've got."

Vlak started to get up, but Sully leaned across the table and pulled her back down. "Running is not a good idea. They're armed. I saw a gun."

"Great," said Hutch. "Now what?"

"Be cool," said Sully. "Drink your beer. Don't even look at them. We're just some backpackers, having a beer in the sun."

"I am not having a beer, Hutch."

"Good point, here." Sully pushed his glass across to Vlak.

"Idiot! Have you forgotten what happened last time? That won't be suspicious in any way at all, once she keels over."

The two men reached the far end of the beer garden and turned, still scanning from table to table.

They walked slowly down the aisle between the benches and parasols.

Jed took a quick look back at the car by the entrance. The two men there had moved down the street and were standing outside the entrance to another beer garden. They exchanged a few words and then went in.

"I'm sorry. This was never my intention, to involve you all." Vlak looked across at Sully and Hutch on the opposite side of the table, and then at Jed, next to her.

The men in their beer garden were now three rows away and advancing. They took a long look at a lone Japanese tourist nursing an orange juice and moved on.

"Distraction," said Jed. "Run interference."

"What on earth are you talking about?"

"Normal people, you said. Normal backpackers. She blends right in." Jed looked at Hutch.

"So?"

"So," said Jed. And he turned in his seat to Vlak. "May I kiss you?" He waited a beat for a reply, figured that tacit consent trumped alien capture and probing, and dived right in.

The two men in shades and dark suits reached their table and turned their heads to study them.

Hutch and Sully were sinking pints, with very wide eyes, while Jed had his arms and lips around a girl backpacker who was frankly way above his pay grade.

MIB One raised his eyebrows, and dipped his head to talk into his shoulder mike. Then he and MIB Two moved off and headed for the exit.

Chapter 29

Urgent communication (Level: Classified)
To: Director (Europe), Bureau of External Visitor Incursions (BEVI)
From: Professor James Storm, Head of Operations, BEVI Research Unit (Germany)

'Chief – further examination of the craft has confirmed Athens as the most likely destination for Matey. Coordinates point to an end location on the Acropolis where the Parthenon stands [*mapping attached*].

Current hypothesis is that Matey expects to find something of help or value at the site. I mean, he's not going there on holiday, is he? There is coded information on the retrieved hardware which may give some clue – the astro-linguists are working on it now and will update in due course.

I've also shared the Athens coordinates – although no further information – with a friendly source in the

History department at King's College, London. In particular, I've asked for evidence of unexplained natural or other phenomena in the historical record, dating back to Classical times.

Given our working hypothesis, it may be that there have been previous visitors – until now, unrecognised. This would provide a compelling reason for Matey's apparent journey.

As for the craft, it's proving difficult to gain more than peripheral access to its drives and files. Early days yet, I know – and to be fair, we're dealing with entirely new physics and logic-systems.

It's fascinating stuff – just wish we could hot-wire the thing and crack it wide open, but we're conscious of the dangers of going too far, too fast. We all remember what happened at Roswell B, so we're taking it slow and steady. No one wants another hole in the ground.'

———

Voice recording, Prague, Czech Republic:

X-Team agent
- I'm talking to the boys in Berlin now, and we have a CCTV hit on a possible Matey exiting the main station. Trouble is, I have at least half a dozen other possible sightings at various stations from Prague onwards, and nothing concrete has turned up yet. I don't think Berlin will be any different.

The Wrong Stop

Head of Operations, BEVI Research Unit
[response unavailable]

- Really, the Yanks are in the game? What's tickled their fancy?

[response unavailable]

- Well, that makes everything a bit more complicated. Don't suppose they're in a mood to share?

[response unavailable]

- Guess not, thought I'd ask. How come they've arrived pronto in Berlin? Have they got intel we haven't?

[response unavailable]

- Fair point, I don't suppose you would know what their secret intel might be, given that it's a secret. They didn't get the craft, though, right? Or anything from the Plzeň site?

[response unavailable]

- Well, then, all they've presumably got is a satellite track on the downed craft and then traces of us scurrying around central Europe in the dead of night. They're fishing.

[response unavailable]

- Let's hope you're right and they're fishing in the wrong place. I really don't want to lose Matey to Uncle Sam. But, yes, it all points to Athens, I agree. Can't see that Matey could master interstellar flight but then manage to go the wrong way to Greece. That would make them a pretty crap alien, if so.

[response unavailable]

- All I'm saying is, the number of times we chase alerts like this, and it's always some alien that's supposed to have crash-landed on the planet. Never executed a lovely, straightforward landing and stepped out to greet us. Can't they drive or something on Alpha Centauri? Maybe they just send the learner-drivers out to have a look at us.

[response unavailable]

- Sure, I get it, no hands on the steering wheel. You really like that whole tentacle joke, don't you? Tell you what, I'll do a final sweep here in Prague, concentrate on the station. If nothing turns up, we'll pull out tomorrow and head south for Greece.

Chapter 30

"All right, Romeo, they've gone."

Hutch leaned across and tapped Jed on the shoulder. He pulled back with a start, looking dazed, while Vlak remained impassive on the bench next to him.

"Earth to Jed."

Hutch waved a hand in front of Jed's eyes, which seemed to swim slightly and then regain focus. He blinked and swallowed a few times.

"First kiss?" said Sully, sweetly. "Our little boy's all grown up."

"Fuck off."

"First alien kiss," said Hutch. "Is that even legal? You probably should have applied to the United Nations for permission."

"And how was that for you, Vlak? On behalf of humanity, we apologise sincerely. That must have been terrifying."

"It was – interesting," said Vlak. "An interesting exchange."

"That's one word for it!" crowed Sully. "Looks like you've broken him."

Jed was still looking somewhere into the middle distance, with the sort of bemused expression a man might have if he'd walked through a revolving door only to find himself back outside on the street again.

"The stars ... and that black, swirling ..." he said, before adding, "I feel a bit sick."

"I was not prepared for our exchange," said Vlak. "When you – connected with me, I was thinking about the current impossibility of making my return journey home. The route is convoluted and involves a wormhole interchange, so I can see that exchanging neural connections might have been a little disconcerting for you."

"I hope you used protection," said Sully. "Jed can't possibly look after a little alien baby."

"Fuck off, will you," said Jed, but in a strange, uncertain voice.

"They've gone now, anyway," said Sully. He'd watched the two men leave, join up outside with their colleagues, and roar off in the unmarked car.

"Do you think they were looking for Vlak?" said Hutch.

"Pretty bloody coincidental, if they weren't. And they didn't exactly look like regular police. Real MIB vibe. Dark suits, shades, guns. The whole Will Smith."

"I reckon Jed's had his own flashy thing moment.

Did you look into the light, mate? What's the last thing you remember?"

"Snogging your mum," said Jed, irritably.

"You have conducted an exchange with Hutch's mother as well, Jed?" said Vlak. "For what purpose?"

"Bugger off, all of you. I didn't see anyone else coming up with a plan. I just acted quickly, that's all."

"You leaped on her, you old rogue. Been practising on the orcs in Nerd-Soc, have we?"

"It's all right, Jed," said Vlak. "Now that we are enmeshed, I will be able to spawn. Do you have a convenient receptacle?"

She leaned over and peered seriously at one of his side pockets, as Sully and Hutch cracked up. "Humour," she explained to a flustered Jed. "If we really were to be enmeshed, I would have to eat you afterwards."

"So, now what?" said Sully, when he'd stopped laughing. "Now that Athens is a bust?"

"We should get out of here," said Hutch. "Then figure something out." He looked across at Vlak. "I know you said you needed those devices, whatever they are, but there must be something else we can do?"

By now, Jed was looking slightly less bilious, and even reached for what was left of his beer.

"Maybe we don't need to," he said. "Get out of here, I mean. They've been here and searched, haven't they? They're not going to come back any time soon. It's probably as safe here as anywhere, for now."

"OK," said Sully. "Makes sense, I suppose. Right then, let's get some more beers and some food."

Vlak picked silently at her chips, while the others exchanged concerned glances. No one really wanted to be the first to state the obvious – that she was buggered. And if they were honest, they had been relying on Vlak to have the ability to save herself. But now those cards seemed to be off the table, the reality of the situation was dawning on them all. She was buggered and, by extension, so were they, if they all continued to stick together.

It was only a matter of time before shadowy security forces, with far more resources than they possessed, would track them down.

"What were those devices?" said Hutch, breaking the silence. "The things at the Parthenon?"

"To be used for emergency evacuation to the nearest wormhole interchange," said Vlak. "Transportation devices, left for such a situation. They were the only way off this planet, now that I no longer have my ship."

"How did they work?"

"What does it matter? They no longer exist."

"I don't know. Maybe you can use something else instead?"

Vlak gave a half-smile – of resignation, perhaps – and shook her head.

"There is no equivalent technology on this planet. How could there be? Your civilisation is in its infancy."

Sully took offence on behalf of Planet Earth. "Well,

we managed to build something like the Parthenon two and half thousand years ago!"

"Exactly."

Both Sully and Vlak sat back, convinced they had made their point.

Meanwhile, Hutch wasn't letting go of the idea. "Some kind of teleportation device, was that it? We've invented those, surely? I've seen them on the telly."

"In *Star Trek*, you idiot." Jed scoffed at the very idea. "Captain James T Berk reckons we can teleport you, Vlak!"

"The devices are matter transmitters, yes. A fairly simple design, for single-use only, enabling transfer to the local wormhole step-base for onward transport. They are quite elegant." Vlak sounded wistful. "I should have liked to have seen them."

She prodded a button on her smartwatch-help and flicked another image onto Sully's phone.

Two gold circles – shining with a deep intensity – hovered above a black background, and then rotated as a 3D image, showing the circles from all sides and angles.

Each was a thin band, perhaps two inches wide – like a bracelet or bangle – with a slender inset on one side that resembled a slice of dark, polished stone. As the image rotated again, tiny hieroglyphic markings became visible on the interior of each band, while two adjacent, slightly indented, hollows could just be made out.

"They remain inert until placed in close proximity

to a help," said Vlak, brandishing her wrist. "To prevent accidental sequence-engagement, although that was perhaps a redundant refinement for such a planet." Her face betrayed little emotion, but there was a hopelessness in her voice that was hard to miss.

"Cool," said Jed, leaning across to look. "You'd never know it was alien tech. I suppose that's the point."

"Those are the transport thingies?" said Hutch. "Are you sure?"

He took another, closer look as the images turned again – at the deep gold of the bracelets, with their single interruption on one side that resembled a polished slice of onyx.

He was right, he was sure of it.

"You're not going to believe this, but it's your lucky day, Vlak. I know where they are."

Chapter 31

Assignment, Ethics in History Module, Degree in Liberal Arts [downloaded by Corey Hutchinson – assignment completed, Grade 65 percent]:

'The British Museum is a repository and guardian of global culture. But much of its collection could be regarded as "the jealously-guarded booty of a faded imperial power" (Professor Mary Beard).

Select an item from the museum's collection and examine the role of empire in its acquisition and display.'

―――

Information panel at the Parthenon, Athens, Greece:

'The rich sculptural decoration that once adorned the temple of Athena – the Parthenon – has long been removed. This includes the sculpted frieze that ran around the whole building, the sculpted panels above the columns, and the tableaux of life-sized figures that adorned the gable ends, or pediments.

Much remains here in Athens, at the Acropolis Museum, and there are other sculptural pieces held at various museums in Europe.

The most significant collection, of course, is at the British Museum in London – the so-called 'Elgin Marbles,' removed from the Parthenon in the years after 1801 by Thomas Bruce, the Seventh Earl of Elgin. At the time, Athens was under Ottoman rule, and Elgin served as the ambassador of Great Britain to Constantinople (1799–1803).

Elgin had official permission to conduct research at the Parthenon, though whether this permission extended to removal of the sculptural decoration has long been disputed. Whatever the truth, Elgin took possession of large sections of the frieze and other sculptures, and – later facing bankruptcy – he sold them to the British government in 1816.

There is, however, no such dispute about the two golden bracelets (the so-called 'Elgin Bands'), which Elgin also discovered during his research, buried under fallen masonry. His permit explicitly instructed that finds 'of a precious or semi-precious nature, including, but not limited to, any treasures associated with the temple of Athena' should become the property of the Ottoman court.

Instead of handing them over, Elgin – or possibly his agents, without his prior knowledge – secreted the bracelets inside a sculptural plaster cast and transferred them to London.

The 'Elgin Bands' remain on show at the British Museum today, together with the 'Marbles,' and have been the subject of a vigorous debate about cultural ownership ever since.'

―――――

Catalogue entry, British Museum, London:

'Object type – bangle, bracelet

Made in – Egypt?

Found/acquired – Greece (Classical)

Description – Gold bracelets of fine work, with onyx (?) inset

Curator comment – Much about the 'Elgin Bands' remains a mystery. The only certainty is that they were discovered at the site of the Parthenon and removed at the same time as the sculptural friezes.

Investigations over many decades have thus far failed to attach a secure provenance to the two bracelets.

They are not Classical Greek in appearance, and their age is uncertain. It has been suggested they date from Dynasty IV, Old Kingdom of Egypt (2613 to 2494 BC), as they bear hieroglyphic markings (still untranslated) of a related nature – though no other examples are known. The polished stone insets, while resembling onyx, contain a chemical compound that has never been fully identified or recognised.

Their use is also disputed – domestic and ornamental, or perhaps regal and processional?

The fascination, of course, is in their relationship to the Parthenon and, in particular, to the meticulous records kept by the Treasurers of Athena.

The famous stone tablet, dated 434 BC, on display in the Acropolis Museum, Athens, records a 'gift of two bracelets of gold offered by a visiting foreigner.' Although no other treasures from the Parthenon survive, such a gift was not unusual – the Parthenon once housed many valuable items.

The gold bracelets have been connected with this ancient record ever since they were first removed to Britain by Lord Elgin, and later displayed here in the British Museum.

And while there is no direct evidence to link the two, it remains a tantalising notion that in the presence of the 'Elgin Bands' we are able to walk in the footsteps of an ancient visitor – origin and name unknown – who once came to leave a valuable gift at one of the most extraordinary and enduring buildings of the Classical period.'

Chapter 32

Hutch got on his phone, brought up the British Museum website and searched for a catalogue entry.

"There!"

Alongside the description was a gallery of images. Hutch selected one and then laid his phone side by side with Sully's, which still displayed Vlak's transferred image.

They were identical. The Elgin bracelets and the transportation devices were one and the same.

"How is this possible?" said Vlak.

"Because British gentleman used to go abroad and take things that didn't belong to them. I had to do a module on it at college this year. This bloke, Elgin, dug them up at the Parthenon where they'd been buried for centuries, and pocketed them, took them back home."

"And they are now in this building, instead?"

"The British Museum, yes, in London. Where we

live." He gestured at the three of them. "Where we go to college."

"You're sure?"

"It's all here, read it for yourself."

"I cannot – read," said Vlak.

"You what? You can mind-warp ticket inspectors, but you can't read?"

"There is no general requirement on my world for such a basic means of communication. We have other ways of exchanging information."

"No kidding, Jed's still looking a bit green, aren't you, mate?"

"Please," said Vlak. "Tell me what it says."

Hutch read out the accompanying text, while Vlak examined the pictures on the website, paying close attention to the visible hieroglyphs and the small, adjacent dimples on the inner surfaces.

"Those seem to be the devices," she said. "I don't think your scientists have much understanding of matter-transfer protocols if they think that's gold and onyx." She sniggered at the apparent absurdity.

"Well, whatever they are, they're in a case in the Parthenon Galleries in the British Museum. The Elgin Bands, they're famous. About the most famous things in there – along with the Parthenon sculptures, the statue of Ramesses the Great, and the Rosetta Stone. Everyone knows about them."

"I know that last one," said Jed. "Aliens inscribed three ancient languages on a stone, each unlocking the other, so that when humans were ready, they would be able to understand the secrets of the universe."

"Obviously bollocks," said Hutch.

"Let's ask Vlak, why don't we?"

"It is bollocks, I'm afraid, Jed. Your friends on the videos must be mistaken again. I'm not sure their information is entirely reliable."

Sully picked up his phone. "It's two o'clock now. What time's our train tonight?"

The Brussels night train was at 22.56 – almost nine hours away. They had a sleeper compartment booked, and then a change at Brussels in the morning for the Eurostar back to London.

The last full day of their trip. Sully had rather imagined they'd be spending it trying to avoid going to museums and persuading Hutch to go to the pub instead. Whereas, here they were, in the pub – no problem there – but trying to avoid armed goons in blacked-out vehicles, while hiding an alien.

"Any ideas?" he said.

"We must go to Lon-don," said Vlak. "If that's where the devices are." She had brightened considerably since seeing the photographs of the bracelets.

"I was afraid you were going to say that. It's not that simple."

"You said there was a train? And then we shall go to this – museum?"

"It's a bit more complicated, getting back to England. They don't bother so much here, between countries, but you have to have a passport to get back into the UK. And there's proper security at the Eurostar stations."

"I don't understand these words and concepts."

"You need a pass, a permit, a document, to travel between countries," said Sully.

"Countries?"

"You know, different areas on the planet. Places with different people and customs."

"I thought you were all human?"

"We are. But we all live in separate areas – different countries. You have to have permission to travel from one place to the next."

"Really? Extraordinary. Why?"

"What do you mean, why?"

"It seems unnecessarily complicated, that's all."

"Anyone else want to help me out here?" said Sully. "With the whole how-Earth-works-101?"

"You just do, all right," said Hutch, cutting to the chase. "You won't get to London without a passport, that's just how it is."

"I can manipulate the – inspectors. I've done it before."

"Maybe. But it's not like dodging a train ticket. They'll lock you up if they catch you. It's risky."

"It's risky for me to stay here. I'm stranded without the devices, I'll never be able to leave, and they'll lock me up anyway. I have to go to London, it's my only hope."

"One bit of potential good news," said Jed.

"Go on, we could do with a laugh."

"Think about it. You've been traced here, to Berlin, right? They've got people searching for you?" He looked to Vlak for confirmation. "But they obviously don't know what you look like, or you'd be in an unmarked black car by now with a bag over your head. And they also don't know you're with us, not yet, anyway."

"If I end up in an unmarked car with a bag over my head, I'm going to be very cross with whoever talked to you first on that train," said Sully.

Jed soldiered on, warming to his explanation. "And you were heading to Athens, for the transporter devices? And they're chasing you because they've found your ship, right? And could they have found anything on your ship that would also lead them to Athens?"

Vlak nodded her head slowly, as she understood what Jed was driving at.

"Yes, the navigation interface in the cabin. I'd activated it, to release the coordinates for the devices. They will be able to access that information at least, though probably not much else."

"There you go!" said Jed. "They think you're going to Athens. Which you were until about half an hour ago. We're the only ones who know that you now need to go to London. Unless they figure it out, too, but even so, we've got a head start."

Jed looked at the others with a smile on his face. He could see nodding approval from Sully and then Hutch. Vlak was more inscrutable, but surely that was the hint of a smile, too?

"Unbelievably, I think he's got a point." Hutch sounded surprised. "He might actually be right about something."

"Very good thinking," said Vlak. "The logic makes sense."

"Yeah, nice one, Mr Spock."

Jed sat back, rather pleased with himself, although as he continued to think out loud, he did begin to wonder how much of an edge it really gave them.

"Even if we make it to the British Museum, I'm still not sure how you're going to get your hands on the devices – the bracelets. You can't just go and pick them up."

"They're in a display case," said Hutch. "Right there in the room with the Parthenon sculptures. I've seen them. They'll have security, surely? And there are gallery staff everywhere."

"Let's not worry about all that now, boys and girls." Sully clapped his hands together. "We've got a plan. Let's go to London and see what happens. You never know, Jed might have another brainwave if you snog him a bit more, Vlak. First things first, though – we need to get to the station without being caught."

Chapter 33

For a fugitive at the centre of an international manhunt, it proved surprisingly easy to help Vlak avoid detection for the rest of the day.

Working on the principle of hiding in plain sight – and continuing to bank on the fact that their pursuers didn't necessarily know who it was they were looking for – the four of them stuck to public places with lots of passers-by and tourists.

They crossed the river from the Zollpackhof tavern and used the cover of the vast Tiergarten park, following winding, tree-lined paths into some of the quieter reaches. They filled up on pretzels and more chips from mobile cafés in the park, and at dusk made their way out to the Brandenburg Gate at the eastern end. From there, they blended in with the crowds and headed back across the river towards the train station, Berlin Hauptbahnhof.

Progress slowed as they got closer to the station. It

was noticeably busier at the main entrance, where uniformed staff were checking tickets and passes before allowing people through onto the concourse. A couple of police vans were parked at the edge of the square outside, but at least there was no sign of the blacked-out vehicle they'd seen earlier.

"Here we go," said Hutch. "First test." One he wasn't at all confident about. It could all end in the next few minutes, if Vlak couldn't manage to mind-meld a ticket inspector.

He looked her up and down quickly, before they joined the shuffling queue. With her cap and jacket still in Sully's bag, she looked the part – just one more young person trying to catch her train.

"You know what to do?" he said.

"Don't worry, Hutch. I know what to do."

"Me too," said Jed. He moved forward and grabbed Vlak around the waist. She looked amused.

"All right, Casanova," said Sully.

"Got to make it look real."

"Don't kiss her again, whatever you do, your brain will fall out. Dead giveaway."

They split up, and let Jed and Vlak go first, putting others in the queue between them. Just in case, thought Hutch. At least this way, if Vlak got caught they would see what happened.

In the end, it was something of an anti-climax, though for about ten long seconds Jed had his heart in his mouth as he sailed through the checkpoint and then looked back to see how Vlak was faring.

She exchanged a few words in German with the member of staff, who stood there expectantly for a moment, as other travellers showed their tickets to his colleague and then moved on.

Just as the pause became awkward, Vlak reached forward for his wrist and held his gaze, and Jed saw the guy give a momentary start. In the same movement, she proffered the wrist with her smart-help. He dragged his eyes from hers, saw what he apparently expected to see, and waved her through. Jed was waiting for her a few yards away and grabbed her hand in relief.

They regrouped in the middle of the concourse, checked the departure boards, and considered their next move. It was an hour before the train to Brussels left.

"We've still got to get her on the train," said Hutch. "And look." He pointed discreetly at the escalators leading down to the various platforms, where doubtless more staff awaited. There was a lot more visible security, too, with uniformed police walking the concourse, heads scanning slowly from side to side as they patrolled.

"Let's stay up here until the last possible moment," said Hutch. "Don't want to get trapped down on the platform." He realised he was sweating – not only from the warm summer night. And this had just been the easy part, he reminded himself.

Jed took himself off and came back a few minutes later with a plan.

"Side gallery," he said, pointing to the far edge of

the concourse. "Not far from the escalator to our platform, but it's not on the way to anywhere else. Station offices, by the looks of things. Closed this time of night."

They made their way there quickly, in twos, between patrols, moved a little way up the gallery and ducked behind a wide pillar. Hutch and Sully put down their backpacks and they all slumped to the floor – behind them the dead-end of a corridor to station offices, and in front, just around the corner, a view out to the concourse.

Sully opened the top of his pack, lifted out Vlak's cap and jacket, put them to one side and rooted around, looking for something.

"Towel," he said, to inquisitive looks. "Toothbrush, toothpaste. Want them handy at the top of the bag, for the train. You need to get in those toilets straight away, because they get pretty disgusting later on. Don't you remember the overnight train from Paris?"

They all shuddered. There had been water flowing down the corridor by the time they had reached the south of France. And not water from the tap, either.

"How long?" said Hutch.

"Forty-five minutes, until it goes."

"Pretzels?" said Jed, rummaging about in a remote pocket, emptying various items onto the floor as he went. "Sure I had a couple left."

"Time?" said Hutch again, a few minutes later.

"Same as before, minus about two."

"Yeah, sorry."

Jed got to his feet, munching a pretzel, and risked a look onto the concourse. And wished he hadn't, because there suddenly seemed to be a lot of activity over at the main entrance.

Four men in dark suits and dark glasses emerged from the security checkpoint and walked onto the concourse, and then split into twos. Further into the station, they split again, going off in four different directions, quartering the station.

"Bollocks."

"Broken a tooth?"

"Not pretzel bollocks." Jed pointed urgently. "Men-in-black bollocks."

"The same guys?"

"Who knows? Could be. Can't tell the difference with the suits and shades."

They peeked around the pillar and watched the nearest guy make his way slowly across the concourse. He stopped passengers as he came across them and said a few words, showed them something on his phone. There were head-shakes, and sometimes a few more words, before he moved on again. His three colleagues were doing the same across the station; it was very deliberate and very thorough, and there wasn't much of the station left for them to check.

"He's coming this way!" They dived back behind the pillar. "Now what?"

"Don't panic."

"Well, that's not very helpful is it. What else have you got?"

"Hide?"

"Good one. Where?"

"Just look normal, for God's sake. He's going to know something's up if he comes round here and you're all wetting yourselves."

"It's sweat," said Jed, defensively, patting at his shorts. "And I think my water bottle leaked."

They glanced wildly around, gave up any thought of flight, and arranged themselves as best they could. Which meant Jed draping himself around Vlak, and Hutch and Sully busying themselves with something terribly interesting on Hutch's phone.

After an interminable pause, they heard footsteps approaching. Dark suit, dark shades, he peered around the pillar, up the corridor, as if ruling out an area of the station, made to move off, and then spotted the four of them.

"Evening gentlemen, ma'am." Huge, tall, American. Looked like he'd been breakfasting on steroids and could bench-press an SUV. He nodded at them. "Waiting for your train?"

Jed coughed nervously. Hutch took a quick glance at the guy – definite bulge at the waist on one side under his buttoned jacket. That wasn't alarming, in the slightest.

Sully took charge. "Yeah," he said casually. "Just about to go, actually." He reached down for his pack.

"Sure," said the guy. "Hang on a second, though. Take a look at this, will ya?"

He held his massive hand up and flipped his phone open, displaying an image.

"You seen this guy around today? Maybe here, at the station?"

They all looked at each other for a second or two. No one wanted to examine the photo, but knew they had to. The man held the phone out, closer, so that Hutch could see it properly.

Still shot from on high, as if from a security camera, but better definition than the image shown on German TV earlier that morning.

Standing somewhere on a train station platform – Berlin this time, Hutch thought. Earlier today. He recognised the criss-cross of escalators in the background.

Baseball cap with a distinctive flash, zipped-up jacket, face in half-shadow. Could almost be anyone if you didn't know.

If you did, it could only be Vlak.

Chapter 34

Hutch shook his head.

"You sure? Take another look." The man presented his phone again. "And you guys, take a look, please. It's important."

Jed peered over, shook his head, too. "No, sorry."

Sully straightened up, keen to show willing, get rid of the guy. "No, sorry," he said. Then added, "Why? What's he done?"

First rule of subterfuge, Jed could have told him. The spy craft videos were very clear on this. Keep it simple. Never offer more than you needed to.

The guy shrugged. "Police matter. Someone we're trying to trace. You're sure you haven't seen anyone that could be this person?"

"You're not police, though, are you?" said Sully. Cocky Sully. Sully, who should really shut the hell up. "Not German police, anyway?"

The guy took a closer interest in Sully, lifting his

shades, staring him out. "Just doing my job, buddy." He looked around at the little encampment. "What are you guys all doing round here, anyway?"

"Waiting for our train, like we said." Hutch dived in, praying Sully would take the hint and not say anything else.

"Is that so?" The guy took another look at the backpacks on the floor, and the various bits and pieces they'd emptied out.

"And how about you, miss?" he said to Vlak. She had stayed close to the pillar throughout the exchanges and hadn't moved. "You seen this guy?" He stepped forward and held the phone up to her.

"She hasn't. We haven't," said Hutch quickly. "We told you. We really need to get going for our train. We don't want to miss it."

"It'll just take a second," said the guy. He gestured again with the phone towards Vlak. "Miss?"

Vlak raised her head to look at the photo. She held her gaze for a moment, then said, "No, I haven't seen this person."

Hutch could see Vlak looking at the picture of herself, and could see the guy looking at Vlak – even with her hair down, obviously the same person as in the photo, you'd have to be blind not to see it, this close up – and counted out the seconds in his head until the guy twigged.

Instead, he shrugged and snapped his phone shut. "OK, sorry to have bothered you, have a nice day. Nice night. Trip, whatever."

Hutch realised he was holding his breath, willing the guy to leave, and couldn't even look at the others.

The guy turned to go, then paused, his eye caught by something on the ground.

"This your stuff?" he said, indicating the backpacks.

"Erm, yeah, sure," said Sully. "We were just going."

"Hold up," said the guy. He pointed. "Those yours, buddy?"

Vlak's baseball cap. Vlak's jacket. On the ground where Sully had put them, like the big idiot he was.

Hutch was still barely breathing. He was going to pass out at this rate. Jed, he could see to one side, was frozen in a half-crouch, preparing to pick up the few of his own things he'd unpacked.

Sully leaned down and scooped up the cap and jacket, started stuffing them back in the top of his pack.

"Yup, just getting sorted. We'll be on our – "

"Not so fast there, bud. Lemme see." The guy gestured at the pack.

Sully looked up and went for the not-keeping-it-simple-bravado manoeuvre again. "I don't think so," he said. "You're not the police. We've answered your questions, and we're catching our train now."

"Is that so?"

The guy had stepped away from Vlak and had flipped his phone open again. Reached over and pinched the image.

Hutch couldn't see from where he was standing, but he'd like to bet that the man had zoomed in on the image and was checking the suspect's clothing. The guy looked Hutch and Sully full in the face, then turned back to Vlak – studied her closely, too, making up his mind about something.

"That cap and jacket," he said. "Get them out now, let me have a proper look."

Sully wasn't backing down either. "No way," he said. "Come on you lot. He can't stop us. Let's go."

He clipped his pack shut and shouldered it, Hutch too, while the guy took a step backwards and touched his earpiece.

"Bravo, Charlie, Delta," he said. "We gotta situation here. Respond?" There was a squawk of static but no reply.

Sully took a step to his side, as if to go around him. The guy kept his finger to his ear and his eyes on Sully. With his other hand, he lifted his own jacket slightly away from his waist. They could all see the gun in its holster.

"Just relax," the guy said. Then he repeated his call. "Code V, possible," he said. "East side, end of the platforms. Respond?"

"We're going, right now!" said Sully, making a definite move, reaching back for Vlak's hand, nodding urgently at Hutch.

The guy made an equally definite move, hand at his open jacket, hip level. "There's no need for that, fella," he said. "You're going to show me that cap and jacket, and then we're all going to have a little talk. Ow! What the – "

He turned round, as if stung, rubbed the back of his head, and looked at his hand. There was blood on his fingertips.

Jed stood facing him, holding his selfie stick out. It had a stain and a few stray hairs on the top, as if it had just been used to hit a very large, angry American on the back of his head.

The guy looked at Jed, incredulously. As, to be fair, did the other three. Jed, for his part, didn't hesitate. He whacked the guy full in the face with the stick, and then hit him again as the man put his fingers to his now broken and bleeding nose.

"You little fucker!" He roared at Jed, as he dropped to his knees, cupping his face with his hands.

"Some help here," said Jed, advancing again with the stick raised.

"Are you mental?" Hutch couldn't quite believe how to-crap this had gone, quite so quickly. Until a few seconds ago, he'd been thinking they might still be able to talk themselves out of this. No chance now that the Rambo Hobbit had gone to work.

Before Jed could do any more damage – or get them all killed – Vlak appeared in front of the guy. She crouched down to his level and grasped both of his wrists in her hands.

"Look at me," she said.

"I'm going to mess up that little shit," said the guy. "Little alien fucker. He's got green blood, we're gonna see it." He made as if to get to his feet, but then sank to his knees again. His eyes swam.

"That's right," said Vlak. "Listen to my voice."

The man appeared docile for the first time. Blood ran from his nose, dripped on the floor, but he made no attempt to move.

"There is nothing to see here," she said, looking into his confused eyes. "You made a mistake."

"Mistake," he mumbled.

Vlak looked up at the other three. "He won't remember this," she said. "But there are others with him. He called out to them. We need to leave."

"They're getting closer," said Hutch. "They definitely know about you. Even if we run, they're just going to keep coming for us."

"Give them something else to chase, then," said Jed. He was still clutching the selfie stick, poised to use it again if he had to. Adrenaline had got him this far, and it was boosting his mind, too. He knelt down next to Vlak and the guy, now immobile on the floor. "Put them off the scent. Make them think you've already gone south, towards Athens. Can you do that?"

Vlak nodded, understanding. She released one of the guy's wrists and touched his throat. Concentrated for a moment. Then put her fingers to his earpiece and spoke.

It was the guy's voice, coming out of Vlak's mouth.

"Bravo, Charlie, Delta. Code V, definite! Got a lead from some passengers. Seen going down to the platform a couple of hours ago for the Vienna train. Head for the vehicles, go, go!"

Vlak pulled away from the man, and he slumped

back against the pillar. She looked drained, but before getting to her feet she reached for the guy one more time, touched his hand and said, "You tripped over on the way to the vehicle. Very clumsy. Please be more careful."

"Careful," moaned the man.

"Right then," said Sully. "Fifteen minutes until the train goes. Come on, let's get out of here."

Chapter 35

Hutch pulled the compartment door closed and dropped the blinds. The night train to Brussels had left on time and was picking up speed through the Berlin suburbs.

Getting on board had been almost laughably easy, after what they had just been through. They went separately down the escalators as a precaution, but no one on the platform below, or on the train, had so much as looked at their rail passes – though Hutch was sure there would be a check later. They'd worry about that then.

For now, they sat in their private sleeping compartment, already made up into four bunks for the night, and breathed – it seemed to Hutch like the first time for about an hour he'd had air in his lungs.

"Holy shit."

"Word," said Sully.

"But I mean, actual, what the – "

"You're welcome," said Jed.

"Are you kidding! You brained some shady spook built like The Rock."

"With a selfie stick!" Helpless with laughter, Sully could barely contain himself. "Didn't you bring a baseball bat?"

"Idiot! What were you thinking?"

"I was thinking someone had to do something." Jed bristled slightly.

"You could have just snogged Captain America," said Sully. "I thought that was your usual diversionary tactic?"

Hutch was far more indignant. "Or, you could have let Vlak do her Jedi mind trick a bit earlier before you decided to attack him. If that had gone south, we'd all be in Guantanamo being royally probed."

"Yeah, well, I didn't think of that. I just reacted."

"Like some Poundland ninja." Sully guffawed again. "Bloody selfie stick!"

"And he thought you were the alien!" Hutch had just remembered that detail, too. "Though he had just had his nose broken. Probably wasn't thinking straight."

"I have always wondered about Jed, to be fair," said Sully. "But humanity's safe, if all we have to worry about is what's in Star-Berk's pockets."

"Unless that's his extendable probing tool?"

"You're all very funny. If it wasn't for me, they'd still be looking for us. As it is, they're all on the way to Athens. Again, you're very welcome."

"He does have a point."

"Fair enough. Nice one, Jed. Vlak, what do you reckon?"

Hutch looked across to the lower bunk opposite – she was leaning back against the compartment wall, feet stretched out over the bed.

"Vlak, you all right?"

"Yes, Hutch. Thank you. It is – exhausting. That was more than a simple thought transference. Memory wipe, voice synthesis. Those are difficult things to do. I'll be fine, but I need to rest."

"If you can do all that, the rest should be easy. Just Jedi your way through all the checks." Sully brandished an imaginary light sabre, emitting a low buzzing noise through his teeth.

"I do not understand the reference. But the – misdirection is only possible with one person at a time. And they need to be compliant."

"Suppose Jed can't brain every ticket inspector and museum guard we come across?"

"I don't think that would be a good idea." – Vlak looked at Jed – "Although, thank you, Jed, it was very brave."

They were safe, for now. The next stop on the train wasn't until around four in the morning, at the German/Dutch border. If Vlak's ruse had worked, no one should be looking for them heading in that direction, west. With any luck, they were busy shoving photos and guns into the faces of innocent passengers heading south.

Whoever they were.

"Americans," said Sully. "The guy, definitely. His mates, too, presumably? Some kind of X-Files set-up?"

"So?"

"So, nothing. I just like to know who I'm being chased by."

"Brock Anderson," said Jed. "Born Tucson, Arizona." He held up a black passport. "He's got diplomatic status. Figures. Though I don't suppose that's his real name."

"What … where …?"

"It fell out of his jacket, when Vlak was mind-melding him."

"And you stole it? You thought it was a good idea to steal a passport from a massive, ripped, armed alien-hunter?"

"I thought it might slow him down a bit. If he lost his passport, and he needed to show it. Even spies have to go through passport control."

"You stole a passport from a ripped alien hunter *with a gun*? Are you mad?"

"Yeah, about that," said Jed. He reached inside his daypack. "I got this as well. He was out of it, and I thought it might come in useful."

They looked at the handgun. Jed put it on the bed, between himself and Vlak.

"What is wrong with you?" Hutch hissed at Jed. Sully was shaking his head in wonder. "Useful? We're not going to use a gun! That's just asking to get killed. We're already going to get killed, probably, and now you're going to wave a gun around and get us all doubly killed."

"Dude, no one's getting killed," said Sully. "But Jed, that is bonkers. Do you even know how to use it?"

"I could look it up on YouTube – "

"You're not looking it up on YouTube! Put the bloody thing away, before someone sees it!"

Jed picked the gun up, grumbling, and put it back in his daypack.

"We're not keeping it!" Hutch was almost beside himself. Jed was a big enough liability armed with only a selfie stick. He was not being allowed a gun as well.

"What do you suggest? Hand it over to the conductor?" Jed's snarky tone suggested he felt his contribution was not being given the due it deserved.

"Hide the damn thing! Up there." Hutch pointed at one of the top bunks. "Give it here."

He took the gun from Jed and quickly folded it inside one of the thin pillows provided, and then stuffed the whole thing in a pillowcase. He reached up and shoved it in a top corner.

"Unbelievable."

"Maybe you're right," said Jed. "I'm keeping the passport, though. You never know, that might be useful. Bargaining chip, or something, if we get caught."

If? The longer this day had gone on, Hutch had been moving from 'if' to 'when' as far as getting caught was concerned, and the last few minutes had hardly shifted the dial the other way. They had got away with it so far, but they surely couldn't carry on being so lucky? If they had to rely solely on Jed hitting people, or Vlak brainwashing them, Hutch thought they were probably on borrowed time.

"What do you reckon, Vlak?" said Jed. "The passport? Maybe you can use that. You got some kind of pop-up photo-printer in that smartwatch of yours?"

"You really do watch way too many videos," said Hutch, still smarting at the appearance of the gun.

"Yeah, well, a day ago you were taking the piss out of me for believing that aliens had visited Earth and built the pyramids. And here's an alien, visiting Earth, right in our train carriage."

"He has you there," said Sully. "I hate to admit it, but Jed's little video friends were at least right about the aliens."

"She might be an alien, but she didn't build the pyramids. Did you, Vlak?" said Hutch.

"Vlak?"

She had slumped further in the corner, out for the count. Head lolling, her chest rose and fell, and her arms were crossed in front of her.

The boys moved her carefully, so she was lying down, and Jed covered her with one of the blankets provided. And the train clattered on into the night.

Chapter 36

Urgent communication (Level: Classified)
To: Professor James Storm, Head of Operations, BEVI Research Unit (Germany)
From: Director (Europe), Bureau of External Visitor Incursions (BEVI)

'Jim – you'll have seen the reports from Berlin. It seems that Uncle Sam is very much on the case. Source of their intel is unclear, but they took off to Vienna quick-smart late last night. Think we can take this as confirmation that your team is very much on the right track – Berlin is out of the picture and it's all points south we need to be keeping an eye on.

Needn't repeat that it is imperative we acquire Matey first. The Americans only appear to have a small team on the ground, but don't underestimate them – they got that intel from somewhere.'

Voice recording, Vienna, Austria:

X-Team agent
- No sign yet, but they shouldn't be hard to spot.

Head of Operations, BEVI Research Unit
[response unavailable]

- I just mean that if they're anything like the usual Special Alien Ops idiots, they'll be gorillas in sleek suits, shiny shoes and dark glasses. Bloody Yanks, stand out a mile on surveillance. My nan could spot them in the field and she's got cataracts. They'd be far better off dressing like regular alien-hunters.

[response unavailable]

- You say scruffy, I prefer to think of it as 'spy casual.' It's easier to run in combats and trainers. And wearing shades indoors, what's that all about? They must bump into stuff all the time. They're ridiculous. You know what they call themselves, our fine American Special Alien Operations' gang? The A-Team. Tossers, the lot of them.

[response unavailable]

- Look, at least X-Team makes sense for ET chasers.

But A-Team? Honestly, they were all watching the wrong TV shows, if that's what they wanted to be when they grew up. I know where I'd stick that cigar.

[response unavailable]

- Well, if they do bump into Matey first, we'll be on to them. Only four of them by all accounts, last seen racing out of Berlin Hauptbahnhof like someone had set fire to their massive American arses. Don't worry — we've got it covered.

[response unavailable]

- I've got people in Budapest and Bucharest, like we agreed. I'm on my way to Athens next, to set up operations there. If Matey's travelling by train, he can't have got that far yet — but wherever he turns up, we've got people waiting. I'll stick around here in Vienna until the Blues Brothers all arrive, and put a team on them. Can always take them out of the equation if we need to.

[response unavailable]

- No need for an international incident. Just get local law enforcement to nab them for being inappropriately American in a public place. Wearing sunglasses after six pm. Eating too many hotdogs. To be honest, I'd prefer to let them run loose for a bit. If they've got intel we don't have, might as well let them follow it up, and then tag along behind and hoover up the crumbs. Anything else from the craft?

[response unavailable]

- None of it makes any sense. Unless everything in ancient Greece was actually built by aliens, and Matey's just going home?

[response unavailable]

- Because I keep an eye on the usual suspects on YouTube. It's kind of required viewing in our line of work. You never know, one day one of those conspiracy freaks might actually turn up a proper conspiracy. Don't get me started on the bloody pyramids, though.

[response unavailable]

Sure, Prof. Eyes on the prize. I know this is real, don't worry.

Chapter 37

As the hours wore on, no one felt much like sleeping, though Vlak was still dozing – unconscious, inert, switched off, whatever it was.

Hutch had taken the bunk above Vlak – he could feel the outline of the gun in the pillow under his head, which made it even less conducive to getting a good night's rest. He closed his eyes and listened to the regular clatter of train wheels on track.

Jed and Sully were in the two bunks opposite, Sully leaning over from the top to whisper to Jed.

"Home tomorrow," he said. "Today, I suppose, by now. You thought about what we're going to do?"

"Beyond hanging out with an alien and stealing something from the British Museum?"

"I suppose. I don't see how this ends, that's all."

"I'm not sure I want it to. End, that is."

"I like a ridiculous, alcohol-fuelled adventure as

much as the next person, Jed, as you know. But this is a bit full-on, even for me."

Jed was silent. It was full-on. It was also the most excitement he'd had in his life. Ever. He'd been looking for this kind of thing since he was a kid, only none of it had turned out to be real before.

He had wanted it to be, obviously. Three-thousand-year-old helicopter carvings in Egyptian tombs, the Ark of the Covenant as a left-behind alien comms device, spaceship landing tracks in outback Australia, astronaut figures carved on ancient cave walls in Indonesia – Jed had earnestly wanted it all to be true, at one time or another.

But he wasn't an idiot, whatever people said. He knew the video guys were probably full of crap, but he'd never been able to help himself. If there was something real out there, he had wanted to know about it – be ahead of the curve. So he kept watching the videos, just in case.

And now, here it was. Properly real. Genuine. There was an alien in the bed across from him, a pillow with a gun in it somewhere on the top bunk, and an American secret agent with a massive bump on his head and a busted nose where he'd been hit with a selfie stick.

The video guys would cream themselves if they ever got wind of this. Which they never would if the four of them got caught, because the whole story would get buried. As would they, probably in a deep, soundproofed cell somewhere without an extradition treaty. Somewhere with relaxed views on the probity of waterboarding.

The only way this stayed real, Jed knew, was if it had a happy outcome for Vlak. And that's what he decided he was going to try and do – make it end well. Whatever it took.

"Jed?"

"Yeah, I know what you mean. But it's going to be all right, Sully."

"I hope you're right."

Sully retracted his head and eventually nodded off. The next sound Jed heard was Vlak stirring in the bunk opposite. She shook the blanket off and sat upright, swinging her legs over the edge.

"You all right now, Vlak?" said Jed.

"Yes, thank you." She did look better, Jed thought, though it was hard to see in the half-light of the compartment. He peered at his phone.

"Another hour to the first stop," he said. "That will be after four am. Then six-thirty in Amsterdam, and nine-thirty in Brussels."

Vlak looked uncomprehending.

"Cities on the way," he said. "Where the train stops, before we get to London."

"And all these places are different?" said Vlak.

"Sure. Of course. I mean, they're different countries."

"Countries. Yes, you said. Interesting."

Jed wondered if she *was* interested. She said things were interesting, quite a lot, though – for an alien – she didn't actually ask that many questions. That was probably a good sign – after all, if she was out to conquer the planet, or send back intelligence, she would be asking tons of questions. As it was, all she really had a grasp of, after a couple of days on Planet Earth, were the broad outlines of the European rail ticketing system. Jed wasn't sure that would help the Emperor Zorg or whoever with his invasion plans.

Maybe Vlak was more like him – or Sully and Hutch? Just a regular person. A run-of-the-mill alien. Vaguely interested in stuff because, you know, you were a student, and you were supposed to show some interest in what you were being taught and told.

Only, to be honest, at nineteen you didn't know much about anything, and you weren't that bothered about learning new stuff, because it all seemed like a bit of a hassle. You asked a few questions of the tutors to show willing. Turned up to a few lectures. Wrote a few essays.

Not that Jed had even been doing that. For all he knew, Vlak was just another disaffected dropout, with no idea what she really wanted to do – albeit one with telepathic powers and a strong liking for fried potatoes.

Jed realised he had a few questions of his own, if he was ever going to run this as a story on his YouTube channel. Not that he had a YouTube channel yet, but he definitely had a story. A real one, too. The pyramids, for example. That video bloke was clearly talking bollocks after all, and Jed now had proof – an actual alien denial. So, what else could he find out?

"Can I ask you something, how old are you?" he said. He'd been wondering about that, ever since seeing the recently-shot-on-location-in-ancient-Greece video.

"It's complicated," said Vlak.

That was another thing she seemed to say all the time. Jed was beginning to think it wasn't a deflection mechanism. He wondered if Vlak actually knew anything about anything?

"OK. How many years have you been alive then?"

"I'm afraid I can't answer that question, Jed. Universal time doesn't really work like that."

"What do you mean?"

"It's complicated. Your species hasn't yet developed sufficiently to grasp the complexities of the explanation."

"Right." Way to diss humanity, thought Jed, as he tried another tack. "You said that no one has been here for two and a half thousand years. Since the last visitor, who left your emergency transport devices behind? That's a long time."

"If you say so, Jed. Time is, of course, relative. And doesn't really exist in the way you think it does."

OK, maybe Vlak wasn't going to be the star interviewee for his channel. Despite her kosher alien credentials, Jed had nothing he could use so far.

"Your help-device, then?" He reached for her wrist, touching the face of the screen. Authentic alien technology – that had to be worth an explainer video?

"How does it work? The hologram? The translation, all that stuff?"

"It is part of me. It understands my requests." said Vlak. "You've seen it operate."

"No, I mean, how does it actually work?"

"Its core functioning? The neural-drive system? The interface and real-time projection."

"Exactly! All that stuff. How does it work?"

"It is, of course, com – "

"Complicated, I know."

"But also, Jed, I don't know. Not in any way that I could describe satisfactorily."

"You must know! Being hyper advanced, and all that."

Vlak looked at him. "Jed, let me ask you something." She pointed at his phone. "Could you explain to me how your device works?"

He looked at it. "Well, there are chips inside – "

"Chips?" Vlak looked puzzled.

"Not that kind. Micro-processing chips. And then, I guess, it's really like a mini-computer. And then the signal comes from the towers … and that makes the connection for the voice call. And then, with the 5G, there's a … actually, it's more like … right, I get it."

Jed ground to a halt, admitting defeat. OK, so she had a point. The videos always made it look like your average visiting alien knew everything about everything. They'd obviously never met one like Vlak. Which reminded him of one more question that had been nagging at him.

"Why do they call you Vlak?"

"They?"

"Your people. Family, I don't know. Does it mean something in your language?"

"They don't call me that. Vlak is not my name."

Chapter 38

Jed knew they had been through a lot in the last twenty-four hours, but he was sure he had heard correctly, back in the dining car on the way to Prague.

"You said it was! You said your name was Vlak?"

"I apologise, Jed. I misunderstood. Vlak is the name I chose when I arrived."

"You chose Vlak?" He thought back to where they had first met. "What, because it sounded Czech or something?"

"My help takes time to calibrate, when it encounters a new form of communication. 'Vlak' was the first word I heard, as I arrived at the building in – " she searched for the town's name – "Plzeň. I thought it would be useful to have a personal name, if I needed to talk to someone, so I chose that one."

Jed was busy Googling, and he laughed when he saw it.

"*Vlak*, 'train' in Czech. Who knew?"

"I knew, Jed. I thought it appropriate. Isn't 'Train' a suitable name?"

"Names don't really work like that." He laughed again. "It suits you, though. What's your real name, then?"

"You won't be able to pronounce it, Jed."

"Try me."

Vlak paused, then cleared her throat and coughed slightly.

Jed waited. "Changed your mind?"

"I just told you my real name, Jed."

"What?"

Vlak cleared her throat again, almost a gargle, and then gave a faint cough. "I told you it would be impossible to pronounce," she said.

"Very funny," said Jed, laughing. "Wait, you're serious?"

"The naming ceremony is very serious, yes. We carry the name we're given until we return to the cosmic dust."

There was a creaking from the bed above Jed, as Sully stirred and woke. He dropped his head over the side, saw Jed and Vlak talking, and reared back upwards in a coughing fit. Snorted a few times, farted once, and then said, "That's better," as he swung his legs over the side.

"What?" he said, when he saw Vlak's face.

"Sully has just insulted my people most terribly," said Vlak. "And what he had to say about you, Jed, cannot be forgiven." She twitched an eye. Was that an alien wink?

"What?" said Sully again, still waking up. Hutch was moving in the other upper bunk – it looked like he'd dropped off for a while and had woken up now as well.

"We're just talking," said Jed, smiling. He still didn't know whether he believed her or not, but this opened up a whole new line of enquiry.

"I've been thinking," he said. "Are you actually a girl? Woman? Do you even have them? Or men? Sexes, I mean?"

"Whoa, hold on," said Sully. "You can't ask things like that. Didn't you read that freshers' week leaflet?"

"I'm just saying. You look like a girl. An Earth girl, anyway."

"I am Vlak. That is all. We're not configured in the same way as you, it is true."

"You look – configured. Properly, I mean. You know, if you were a girl." Jed tailed off.

"Excellently creepy, mate," said Sully. "Carry on."

Vlak saved him. "This isn't my body," she said. "It is a – simulacrum, I think that's the word."

Jed shook his head, trying to clear the thought that the more she tried to explain things to him, the less he understood.

"It's an image, a representation," she continued. "I needed to assimilate – blend in, as you say – to avoid being captured."

"Where did you get the clothes?"

"I'm not wearing clothes. It's a projection, as is this body. I scanned for suitable models before I left the ship. Your planetary data is not secure, by the way. Anyone can hack into it. You might want to think about that."

"Hang on," said Sully. "I've got your cap and jacket in my bag. You know, the ones that nearly got us killed."

"You're right, Sully. I should have said that the base layer is the projection. The additional outer coverings – I got those at the first transportation building, when I saw that I was going to need more of a disguise."

Hutch listened to all this with mounting doubt. The sort of doubt he'd first had when Vlak had revealed herself to be an alien. He'd got over that, only to be presented with even more outlandish things that barely made sense. He climbed down from his bunk and stood in front of Vlak.

"You're telling us that none of this – you – is real?"

"I am real. And what you see is real to you. I don't understand the concern."

Hutch reached forward. "May I?" He gestured with his fingers and Vlak nodded.

"It feels like clothes," he said, touching the bottom of her T-shirt and then a side fold of her trousers. "They *are* clothes. You're wearing clothes." He gestured again, this time at her hair. "Can I?"

Vlak bowed her head slightly, and Hutch touched her hair. Jed reached out, too, conscious that it looked like they were petting a young woman on the head in a private sleeping compartment, and that couldn't be good, but he really wanted to check this out.

"Hair," he said, rather disappointedly.

"A forcefield," said Vlak. "That's all. And no, Jed, I don't know how it works. It just does."

"You're wearing a forcefield?" said Hutch.

He was still trying to decide if he was going to accept all this. It seemed like an odd line to draw, given all that he had seen Vlak do up until now. But a forcefield? Seriously?

"Technically, it would be more accurate to say that the forcefield is wearing me."

"Well, that makes *all* the sense." Hutch gave up. He hardly knew what was going on anymore. Barely any sleep for two days. Far too much beer, and way too much adrenaline, what with all the running, hiding, and saying WTF all the time. He needed some fresh air. "Going to stand in the corridor a bit," he said, sliding open the compartment door.

The train began to slow down as he stood there, next to the slit of an open window. Hutch could hear the clack-clack of wheels on rails, and then saw the distant lights of a station ahead. It was cooler out here in the corridor, and he pushed his face up into the night air, enjoying the breeze, watching the lights get closer.

Sully was still working through the latest alien-related information, and finding it hard going.

"Just to get this straight," he said. "You're not a woman? Female? Or a bloke? And you picked some random catalogue model and fired up the old forcefield? And none of those clothes actually exist? Apart from a cap and a jacket you lifted off some unfortunate traveller at the station? And you don't really have any hair? Or any – I don't know – " and he held up his hands in exasperation.

"That is all correct, Sully."

"Bugger me."

"Hang on," said Jed. "Do we even want to know what you actually look like?"

"Oh God," said Sully. "It better not be tentacles. I'll bet it's tentacles."

"Or it'll be like those dangly braids and teeth in *Predator*. Freaked me right out when I saw it."

"I don't have tentacles, Sully."

"That's something, I suppose."

"Although it rather depends on what you feel about scales and wings."

"No way! God, nightmare. No offence to your people, obviously. I'm sure they're all lovely."

"It's a joke, Sully. I understand your species' fear of the unknown, the strange and the different, and I have built upon it to construct a humorous remark."

"Very funny."

"Thank you, Sully."

"You don't know shit about sarcasm though."

"Bipedal biology is standard throughout the galaxy. You don't need to worry. I merely tweaked some features to be less conspicuous. And acquired a persona and clothes to blend in."

"I still don't know if you're a boy or a girl."

"Neither do I, Jed. It is unimportant."

"Not here, it isn't."

Light from the corridor flooded into the compartment as Hutch pulled the door open and stepped inside.

"Bad news," he said. "The train's stopped. There are ticket inspectors on the way, end of the carriage. And border guards behind them, checking passports."

Chapter 39

"That's way too many people to mind-meld, right?"

Vlak nodded.

Hutch poked his nose back out of the door and sneaked another look. "You better come up with something because they're halfway down the carriage." He could hear doors being slid open, and raised voices from the inspectors and guards as they roused sleepy travellers.

"She shouldn't even be in here," said Jed. "We only booked for three people. She won't be on their passenger list. It's going to look sus."

"It's going to look even more sus when she shows them an American diplomatic passport with a massive geezer in the photo," said Sully. "Nice one, by the way, Jed."

Hutch ducked back in. "We'll have to hide her."

They all looked around. A four-bunk cabin, the beds already laid out. A pull-down window blind. A fold-out table. A luggage rack with two backpacks in it. There was nowhere to conceal a humanoid alien, which – while regrettable – could hardly be said to be the fault of the train design team.

"Hide her? Righto, genius. Unless she can climb into one of Jed's pockets, we've had it."

Hutch slid the door open a crack and risked another look. The guards were now three compartments away, standing in the corridor, examining passports.

"Isn't there anything else you can do?" said Jed. "Activate a cloaking device or something? Make yourself invisible?"

"No," said Vlak. "I can't do any of those things."

"Maybe she can say she lost her ticket and her passport? It must happen, right?"

"And what would they do? Chuck her off the train? Take her into custody because she doesn't have any documents?"

"How would I know?"

The voices were outside the adjacent compartment now. "Well, we're just about to find out," said Hutch, "because it's us next. Guys – "

He turned to the sight of Jed leaning down and pulling at one of the lower bunks. The daytime train seats folded into bed mattresses for the night, and as Jed lifted the bed up, he revealed a storage space below. There were two more spare pillows in there, and a small pile of folded overnight blankets, still in their plastic wrapping.

"This do?" said Jed. He threw in the American secret agent's passport, helped Vlak to climb in, lowered the bed carefully as she arranged herself inside, and then sat back on the mattress, breathing heavily.

They looked at each other. No one said a word.

"Tickets! Passports!" There was a rap on the door, which then slid open, while the lights in the compartment came on.

The train inspector checked his reservations list and examined their rail passes. He moved on to the next compartment, while two border guards took a look at their passports, holding each photo up to check.

One of them cast his eyes around the compartment. "Your luggage?" he said, pointing up at Hutch and Sully's bags. "Only two?" He gestured at the three of them.

Jed grabbed his daypack from a corner and brandished it. Slapped his hands on his sides to show his ridiculously laden pockets. The guard shook his head in quiet disbelief – as if he'd seen everything now – and beckoned for Jed's daypack. He took a quick look inside – crumpled train map, half a pretzel, phone charger, toothbrush – and handed it back.

Then he gestured at Hutch's pack, up on the luggage rack. Hutch lifted it down for him and put it on the floor. That left the pillow in plain sight – the one with an American secret agent's gun stuffed in it.

Hutch tried desperately not to look up as he unfastened the clips on his backpack for the guard, but the more he thought about not looking at the pillow, the more he was sure he was twitching and rubbernecking.

If he was, the guard didn't notice. He rifled through the top few layers of Hutch's pack – tangled clothes, mostly – and then stood back, flicking his hand to say he'd finished.

That left Sully's pack – the one with a jacket and very distinctive cap in it, currently featuring on 'Germany's Most Wanted.' The cap and jacket that an alien, who otherwise apparently wasn't wearing clothes, had stolen from a Czech student.

The guard looked up at Sully's pack, presumably thought about digging through some more soiled clothing and half-eaten snacks, wondered briefly about his life choices, and then turned on his heels. "Gentlemen," he said, as he exited.

The silence continued for another minute or so, until they could hear the guard further down the carriage. Hutch cracked first.

"I'm going to have a heart attack!"

"Me first," said Sully. "I'd forgotten about that cap. And that bloody gun!"

"And again, you're most welcome," said Jed, as he lifted the base of the bed. Vlak lay curled up inside, and turned her head to the light. "You all right, Vlak?"

"Yes, Jed. Most interesting. You made me invisible." She smiled. "Very clever."

"Let's not go overboard. He stuffed you in a box," said Sully. "We're not going to be able to do that every time. I don't think my heart can stand this."

Vlak climbed out of the storage compartment, and they put the packs up and out of the way again.

"Don't worry, Sully. If your heart stops, I'll be able to start it again," said Vlak, as she sat back on the bed. "At least, I think so – you must remind me which organ is which before I begin. You only have the one heart, correct?"

"See, now I don't know if you're joking or not. I don't really like it either way."

The train gave a lurch, and then started to move forward, picking up speed. For the next couple of hours – now the very early morning, with light beginning to peek through the blinds – they slumped into a doze, largely missing the stop in Amsterdam.

By eight in the morning, they were flashing through the flat fields of The Netherlands and by nine they were across the border into Belgium, with only the final run into Brussels ahead of them.

Jed was already on his phone, buying four seat reservations for the Eurostar train to London, fretting about ticket and passport checks. "We'll be all right with our rail passes," he said. "But Vlak will have to zap someone's brain at least once."

Hutch, by now, was feeling more sanguine. Against all the odds, they had got this far – who was to say they wouldn't make it all the way? He couldn't work out whether he was feeling more Zen about it all, or whether he was just very, very tired, hungry and deluded.

"If I'm honest," he said, "by this point, I don't care

if they lock me in a cell, provided it has a bed and a regular supply of meals. A TV would be nice, but it's not a deal-breaker."

The train pulled into Brussels Midi station at nine-thirty, and they sent Sully ahead to check out the platform. Nothing appeared out of the ordinary, so he signalled to the rest of them through the window and they came out quickly, flanking Vlak, and moved down the escalators into the main concourse.

"Three hours until the London train. So now what?"

In the end, they waited across the main road from the station in a brasserie that was open for breakfast. In Sully's case, that also meant a beer, just because he could and it would apparently be rude not to, it being Belgium. "It's flavoured with strawberries," he pointed out. "It's basically fruit. It's a breakfast beer."

And it really did seem as if the fates were with them, once they braved the security checks at the Eurostar terminal.

Their ticket barcodes got them through the first scanner – Vlak simply following suit with a cloned version on her smart-help. The bags went through the X-ray machine with no trouble, though Jed had to divest himself of almost everything he was wearing before he was allowed past.

There was a heart-in-the-mouth moment at passport control, when Vlak – coached by the others – presented the American agent's passport. As she handed it over, she appeared to fumble and made sure she brushed her fingers against the officer's hand. He looked up, and then appeared startled as she grasped his hand and looked into his eyes.

There was a flicker between them, and then an interminable pause as he looked intently at the passport photo of a thickset man with a buzzcut, and then straight into the eyes of a young woman with fine features and tousled brown hair.

"Thank you," he said, and Vlak moved past the booth to join the others.

"This way," said Jed. "London, here we come."

Chapter 40

Urgent communication (Level: Classified)
To: Professor James Storm, Head of Operations, BEVI Research Unit (Germany)
From: Director (Europe), Bureau of External Visitor Incursions (BEVI)

'Jim – thanks for the suggestion from your X-Team guys. I had Uncle Sam's little tag-team picked up in Vienna in the end.

Seems they were frightening passengers at the main station with some fairly aggressive questioning, so we asked local authorities to have a quiet word. It soon escalated, when one of them couldn't produce ID – and he was sporting some hefty cuts and bruises, too. Reckoned he'd 'fallen over' – make of that what you will.

Anyway, they are in Vienna Central in a holding

room. The US Embassy is already making waves, but nothing we can't handle. I don't think they have a clue what the four musketeers were doing in Berlin and Vienna, anyway – there's not much love lost between the State Department and the Area 51 boys.

They're out of the picture, though. Matey's not going to fall into American hands. You should have a clear run to Athens – so, Jim, don't let me down. Let's find him and bring him in.'

———

Incident report, European Sleeper service, Berlin to Brussels, arrival 09.26:

'Cleaning crew on their regular duties earlier retrieved a hazardous item, hidden on board the above service – Carriage D, Compartment 3.

Item – one firearm (type, pistol), discovered wrapped in a sleeper-issue pillowcase.

It was handed to the railway police on duty at Brussels Midi, who have secured it pending the arrival of the regional crime unit. Anti-terrorist authorities have also been notified.

The staff in question have been debriefed. They remain at Brussels Midi and have been excused further duties today in case they are required for questioning.

There is no suggestion that any of the cleaning crew are involved; all are reliable staff, of long service. Other train staff from the overnight service are currently being contacted and will be interviewed in due course.'

Voice recording, Athens, Greece:

X-Team agent
- You what? Say again?

Head of Operations, BEVI Research Unit
[response unavailable]

- In Brussels? A gun? They're sure it's US spook-issue?

[response unavailable]

- And we've still got the four A-Team jokers under lock and key in Vienna?

[response unavailable]

- Only three guns and three passports between the four of them, you don't say. Well, this puts a bit of a spin on things. Don't suppose they're talking?

[response unavailable]

- No, to be fair, I wouldn't in their position. Just sit tight and wait for the man from the embassy to spring me, no questions asked. So, what are you thinking? That the gun in Brussels is something to do with Matey?

[response unavailable]

- Berlin didn't make sense, Brussels makes even less. All in the wrong direction. I've got people in every major train and bus station between Budapest and Greece – we know which way Matey's heading, and I'm waiting for him. With a kebab, by the way, bloody good.

[response unavailable]

- I hear you. No, I can't explain how some Spook Academy idiot loses his gun in Berlin and it ends up in Brussels. What about his passport?

[response unavailable]

- He can't explain that either. I'll bet he can't. It's not a good look for him, is it? Maybe if he took his stupid dark glasses off, he'd be able to find it.

[response unavailable]

- All right, tell you what, get someone in Vienna to have another quiet word before their embassy guys get there. Maybe he can be persuaded to talk? And let's have our people in Berlin and Brussels take a look through the security footage at the stations, just in case. But it doesn't feel right to me. I mean, I don't set any great store by their alien special-ops guys – they only got the Area 51 stuff because the damn spaceships virtually fell on them in Roswell. It wasn't anything clever they did. You say Matey's going to Greece, I believe you.

Chapter 41

The clinching argument was the prospect of a hot shower and a massive bowl of Cheerios.

Jed was for going straight to the museum, as was Vlak, for obvious reasons. But as Sully pointed out, the Elgin Bands – the bracelets, the devices – had been in the museum for over two hundred years and weren't going anywhere. Plus, no one else knew their real importance. Double-plus, they didn't have a plan yet. And plus-squared, Sully was heartily sick of carrying his pack around after three weeks on the road.

"Let's go back to the flat, dump the stuff. Have a shower, get something to eat. What time does the museum close?"

Jed was already on it. "Eight-thirty tonight – late-night opening."

"There you go then. We can regroup for a bit, and then go and do a recce. We're going to need to have a look first and figure out how to get hold of the bracelets. It's not like we can just walk in and pick them up."

They were really doing this, then? Hutch was running on pure anxiety by now, with a headache worse than any hangover. A shower sounded amazing, and the Cheerios hardly any less so. After that, if he was still standing, then sure – a trip to the British Museum on a warm, summer's night with their new alien friend, why the hell not?

The flat was in Islington, around the corner from Angel tube – one quick stop on the underground, once they'd got out of St Pancras station and followed the signs for King's Cross.

It had the look and smell of a place that ordinarily housed six nineteen-year-old boys who had forgotten to clean up before they all went away for the summer. Pizza boxes still tottered on the kitchen counter, while there was stuff growing in the sink that would probably be able to talk to Vlak, given another few weeks of microbial growth.

They cleared a space for her on the sofa and she watched, both uncomprehending and amused, as they dropped their packs and made themselves at home.

"You – live here?" she said, looking around.

"Six of us altogether," said Sully. "The other three are still away. My room's there." He pointed down the hall. "Jed's next door, Hutch at the end."

"You live – in these small spaces?" Vlak elaborated, as though she hadn't been understood. "With these personal items?" She gestured equally at the pizza boxes, the TV, the armchair, a pair of battered trainers sticking out of a wastepaper basket, and the outsized box of Cheerios on the kitchen table currently being upended by Hutch. "What's that interesting smell?" she said, sniffing at the teenage-boy-infused room. "I cannot detect its constituent parts."

"What smell?"

Jed had disappeared inside his room on arrival, from where they had heard an almighty clunk. He emerged now clad only in boxers and a T-shirt.

"Thank God for that," he said. "The relief. Those travel trousers – I think I took too much stuff."

"You think?"

"Yeah, I'm going to travel light from now on. Twin-pocket cargo shorts only."

"The lesson you have taken from all this is that pocket-travel is a good idea, only you should limit yourself to two side pockets?"

"Exactly. I never used my AeroPress, for example. Right, I'm going to have a – "

"Dibs on the shower," yelled Hutch, and he squeezed past Jed and slammed the bathroom door.

"Rude," said Jed. "Hate it when he does that." And then, "Sorry," to Vlak. "You can go before me, if you like."

"Thank you, Jed, but it will not be necessary. My forcefield has a self-clean function."

"Up to you, but I just want to feel properly clean again."

Vlak held a finger in the air, licked it and then stuck

her tongue out and retracted it. "Your planet has a very challenging environment. Dihydrogen-monoxide alone won't clean your skin of the polycyclic aromatic hydrocarbons, the volatile organic compounds, the sulphur dioxide, the particulate matter, and – " she licked her finger one more time, "ah yes, the ozone. It will not make you properly clean. But of course, if it makes you feel better, you should have a shower. And then we'll go to the museum, yes?"

Sully wandered off to his own room, eating from a bowl as he went. He kept half an ear out for the shower, so he could duck in before Jed, too, and tipped most of the clothes out from his pack onto the floor. He saw Vlak's cap and jacket and kicked them into a corner – better they weren't seen outside anymore.

An hour later, they had all showered and eaten something, except for Vlak, who hadn't moved from the sofa. She had refused a glass of tap water, after expressing surprise that the flat didn't have a dedicated distillation unit. And she was currently engaged in examining the small print of the Cheerios box, inputting the nutrition values into her smart-help, and looking appalled as Jed helped himself to a second bowl.

Sully had found her a bucket hat, in case they thought she needed to cover up again, and Hutch had donated an old denim jacket he'd been meaning to try and sell. She tried them on in front of the boys, and they agreed that it definitely changed her look. Maybe she'd need them, maybe she wouldn't, but they might buy her some time if they had to run again.

Sully took one last look around his room. The others were in the lounge, waiting to go – and, like them all, he had no idea how this was all going to turn out. It was going to be some story, whatever happened. He just hoped he'd be in a position to tell it to the rugger boys. They wouldn't believe him, of course, but it might shut them up for a while about Ayia Napa.

He noticed Jed's door was half open as he walked past, and he glanced in. He only stopped walking because it seemed odd. Apart from the clothes Jed had obviously kicked off when he'd arrived, the floor was clear and the room was suspiciously clean. No one in this flat was *that* tidy.

Sully gently pushed open the door. He could still hear the others talking in the lounge against the murmur of the television.

Jed's room was packed up. It must have been done before they had left on their trip, because he certainly hadn't done it in the last hour or so.

There were sealed boxes on the bare desk, and a couple of suitcases and a filled, stripey laundry bag on the stripped bed. No posters on the walls. None of his little action figures, sorry, collectibles, on the shelf. A 'Star Wars' cushion perched on top of a rolled rug. Everything packed away and ready to go.

Which made no sense at all, because term started again in three weeks' time, and this was where Jed lived. Where they all lived. Where they had all agreed to stay on for the coming year.

He pulled the door shut quietly. There was a story there, too, no doubt, and he'd have to ask Jed about it. Not least because if Jed was moving out, him, Hutch and the others would have to find someone else to move in. And Jed, for all his idiosyncrasies, was actually quite a good bloke to live with, seeing as he rarely came out of his room or bothered anyone else.

Sully shook his head. As if he didn't have enough to worry about right now.

"Ready?" Jed spotted him hovering in the corridor, and Sully walked on through. The TV was on, Hutch flicking through the news channels.

"Anything?" They all knew what Sully was asking.

"If you mean, is there an alien on the run in Europe and, by the way, have you seen these three likely lads, because we'd quite like to catch them and give them a good probing as well, no, nothing."

"That's good news, right?"

"I suppose. If the dark forces of the deep state are after us and Vlak, I'm not sure they'd be announcing it on the telly. They might be watching us right now, for all we know. Parked up outside in a van, waiting to pounce."

"Paranoid, much? God, you're as bad as Jed."

"Just realistic. Pessimistic. I don't know. I've never been on the run before."

Chapter 42

They moved quickly away from the flat, looking around nervously for any signs of panel vans with tinted windows or large men in shades loitering by lampposts. Figuring it was safer to stay off transport they walked to the museum, cutting through back streets towards Russell Square, and picking up takeaway fish and chips on the way.

They found a bench in the Russell Square gardens and ate out of cartons, watching people come and go. Kids kicking a ball, a few tourists, some people on their way home from work.

"This is enjoyable," said Vlak, as she finished off her meal. "I'll miss chips. And your sun is warmer than mine."

"Worth getting off at the wrong stop for?" said Jed.

"What do you mean?"

"You know, crashing your ship. Landing on Earth by mistake. Getting on the wrong train."

Vlak seemed to consider the question seriously. "I doubt these chips are worth the value of my ship. But your planet is more surprising than I had first thought."

They finished up and walked south through the gardens, stopping just before the exit, where a man standing on a wooden crate was haranguing passers-by. He wore a close-fitting silver helmet – tinfoil had been used in its construction – and was holding a small plastic box crisscrossed by wires, with a homemade coat-hanger aerial sticking out of the top.

"Aye aye, one of your mates, Jed."

"They are already here!" The man was shouting and waving the box around. "The government don't want us to know! Shut out the radio waves, turn off the TV, the internet. You'll see I'm right! When you shut out the noise, you'll see the truth. They are among us! I can detect them, I know they are here!"

"This is you, Jed, one day, if you're not careful. Starts off with the videos, and before you know it, you're on a box in a park."

"Sod off."

"Is this man really one of your friends, Jed?" Vlak looked curious.

"Of course not. He's just a loony."

"They want us to think it's crazy," shouted the man. "They try to hide the truth with their fake news and gameshows, with their weapons of mass distraction. There's no reality in reality TV – MasterChef is just a tool of the Illuminati! You're being lied to, but the truth is out there. There are aliens among us. They are here. I see them!"

"He seems very well informed," said Vlak.

"He does at least have his trousers on," said Sully. "It's not always a given with these blokes, hey Jed?"

"They are here, I tell you!" The man was beside himself now, waggling his plastic box and hopping up and down on his crate. "They are among us!" Spittle sprayed as he shouted, and people hurried on past, avoiding eye contact.

"Yes," said Vlak, stepping forward. "Indeed, here I am. How does your machine work, I am very interested?"

"Unbelievers!" shrieked the man. "Mockery, ridicule! The last refuge of a blind planet! Of course, you fools can't see it! But they are here, among us now!"

"Vlak, come on!" Hutch pulled at her arm. "He's just a nutter."

"Was Jesus a nutter?" yelled the man. "Was Einstein? Is Ron Perlman? Lady Gaga? They are all among us I tell you! They have always been among us!"

"I don't know these people, "said Vlak, "but perhaps they can help me? I have my own device – "

"Government stooge!" screamed the man. "Truth-denier!" He rubbed his tinfoil hat energetically. "Must drown out the noise!"

"Vlak, seriously! Are you trying to draw attention to us?" They pulled at her arm, and left the park, the man still bouncing and shrieking on his box.

"There is never a dull moment," said Sully. "I'll give you that."

"I thought he'd be happy to know that he was right," said Vlak. "He seemed very certain about everything."

"For God's sake!" Hutch pulled them all into a circle on the pavement, outside the park. "We've just spent two very stressful days trying to get here undetected. We're just around the corner from the museum. Do you think we can manage to get there without riling any more loonies?"

"I feel sorry for him," said Jed.

"You would."

"I don't mean that. I mean, he's obviously bonkers. But for the only time in his life, probably, he's right. An alien literally talked to him, and he wouldn't have it."

"I could go back," said Vlak. "Perhaps show him my – "

"No!" They grabbed her arm and steered her away, down Montague Street and then round the corner onto Great Russell Street. A long, wrought-iron fence ran along the street to the British Museum's main entrance, where a queue snaked from the gateway into the main courtyard.

They stood in line in front of the high columns and sculpted pediment of the main building, and shuffled towards a marquee where museum staff were checking bags. The search seemed very perfunctory and it was the first time for days that any of them had felt no apprehension about a security check. As long as Vlak kept it together for just a little longer.

She seemed to have other things on her mind, though. "Are all important buildings on your planet built the same way?" she said, looking at the museum façade.

"How do you mean? Oh, right, like the Parthenon?" said Hutch. "No, good spot. It's just your standard cultural imperialist design for housing stolen items."

"Ooh, get Che Guevara. Been copying stuff off Wikipedia for your essay, at all?"

"I may have browsed the internet for a while, it's true. Got sixty-five percent, though. You may not be familiar with such a mark. It's like when you get a smiley face on one of those crayon maps you draw in your seminars."

They breezed through security – no bags to check, even Jed had resisted stuffing his pockets with the usual junk – and made their way round to the broad steps under the columns.

"The devices are in here, Hutch?" For the first time, Vlak looked uncomfortable. "You're sure?"

"Definitely. Or at least, they were a few months ago when I was here, and they've been in the museum for a couple of centuries, so don't worry."

"This is the only opportunity I have to go home. That's all. I'm nervous."

"You and me, both, Vlak. And just because they're

here doesn't mean we can get at them. Still haven't figured out that bit yet."

"Haven't you got a laser beam or something?" said Jed. "Or some sucky space device that you can use to whoosh them out?"

"Sucky space device?" said Vlak. "I think Hutch is right, you watch too many of those videos."

"Smash and grab, then?" said Jed. "Vlak does her stuff and pouff, she's gone. Right, Vlak?"

"Almost, Jed. It is a bit more complicated than that, but it shouldn't take long."

"Yeah, well, we're not smashing and grabbing, boys and girls," said Sully. "Not if the three of us want to stay out of prison. Be all right for Vlak, off back home, but I don't want to be sat on by some hefty security guard while they call for the police."

"Too right," said Hutch. "Today, we're just scouting things out." He looked sternly at Jed. "No smashing. No grabbing. OK?"

"Fine, whatever."

"OK, then." Hutch turned to Vlak. "We've got an hour before it closes. Ready? Let's go and find you a way to get home."

Chapter 43

Transcript from BEVI interview, Vienna, Austria

Subject – Debrief of American operative, Brock Anderson (BA)

'BA: I told you, I lost it. I want the embassy here now.

BEVI: They're on their way, don't worry. Burgers and milkshakes for you, any time now. But just help me out, for the paperwork. We're on the same side.

BA: Sure, if you say so.

BEVI: Well, maybe not the same side. But after the same slippery visitor from afar, shall we put it like that?

BA: I've no idea what you're talking about, but whatever you say, bud.

BEVI: Come on, this doesn't look great for you. Picked up on an unclassified op in Europe that wasn't cleared through us. Lost your gun. Lost your passport. Broken nose. Covered in blood. Bit careless, aren't you?

BA: I told you, I fell over.

BEVI: Well, sure, if you say so.

BA: Look, bud, I don't know what you want from me. I got my orders, you got yours, and never the twain shall meet.

BEVI: Aren't you at all interested in how your firearm ended up in Brussels? The passport, we haven't found yet, but it's only a matter of time.

BA: Brussels?

BEVI: Yes, interesting isn't it? All of us looking towards Athens, and yet –

BA: If you say –

BEVI: Yes, I know, if I say so. Well, I do. Do you think that maybe you did stumble on something? Don't you want to know? I mean, this is huge. Bigger than anything, if it's true. Instead of just being the idiot who lost his gun and his passport on a mission, you could be part of it. Help me out here.

[pause]

BA: I honestly don't remember. Nose is killing me. Got a goddammed headache that won't go away, and you yabbering at me doesn't help.

BEVI: You were in Berlin, does that ring a bell?

BA: Yeah, Berlin, sure, no big secret. Running an ID query at the station.

BEVI: Go on.

BA: I wish I could tell you. All I remember is, there were these kids –

BEVI: Kids?

[pause]

BA: I dunno, backpackers, students, something like that. They checked out. I mean, I thought they did. There was this one little fucker. Dude with pockets – weird, you know? Something about him.

BEVI: And?

BA: Fuck knows. Next thing I remember, I'm in the car bleeding like a son of a bitch, and we're driving to Vienna. I only found out later I'd lost the gun and passport. We hit the station in Vienna, started checking that out. And the rest you know. Now, is the embassy coming or not?'

———

Voice note, to: Head of Operations, BEVI Research Unit
From X-Team agent, Athens, Greece

'Prof – this is interesting [*transcript attached*], just been forwarded by one of my guys in Vienna. Seems like our careless American friend had an encounter that might or might not be relevant.

Also, take a look at the vid [*CCTV footage attached*, Berlin Hauptbahnhof]. We ran a check, just in case, and what do you know? I'd say that's 'Weird dude with pockets' at 21.37, heading down the escalators for the Brussels night train.

You think this could be Matey? Would possibly explain the gun turning up in Brussels? Though we are all dead set on the destination being Athens, so who knows? Anyway, you want me to follow it up?'

Chapter 44

Hutch led them through the main entrance and into the museum's soaring Great Court, where scores of visitors were still circulating at the end of the day. He was impressed every time he came here, and he could see that even Sully and Jed were taken aback by the sweep of polished limestone flooring, the gleaming, white, central rotunda, and apparent floating glass roof.

Vlak, he was less certain about. She looked around, with a neutral expression, as she had done pretty much anywhere they'd been. Train carriage, student flat, chip van, national museum – he supposed it was all alien to her. She didn't look any more or less impressed than usual, but maybe this shining, majestic hall was the sort of space they parked their hover-scooters, wherever it was she came from.

"This way."

He took them around the lefthand side of the

rotunda and through another portico, passing the display case containing the Rosetta Stone. Jed's eyes widened at that, but Hutch kept them moving, pushing through a tour group coming the other way.

Straight ahead, right down at the end, was the place he was aiming for. The entrance to the main Parthenon Gallery, flanked by two narrow exhibition rooms, one on each side.

Hutch had spent some time here for his assignment, trying to understand the sequence of historic events that had led to some of the world's most famous sculptures ending up two thousand miles from the place they had originally adorned – the temple known as the Parthenon, sited on the Acropolis in Athens.

As for the rights and wrongs, Hutch still wasn't fully committed to an answer – one of the reasons why his sixty-five percent grade mark hadn't been higher. But as they walked into the centre of the long, main gallery, and he spied the 'Elgin Bands' display case at the far righthand side, he knew one thing for certain.

If Lord Elgin hadn't plundered the sculptures – or removed them for safekeeping, if you preferred – then the bracelets might never have been discovered.

Without them, Vlak had no chance of going home. But thanks to a light-fingered, nineteenth-century Scottish nobleman, she was at least still in with a shout.

They moved down the long gallery, past the famous frieze sculptures attached to the walls, where a tour guide was still holding sway. At the end, on a raised dais, were the assembled chunks of statuary from the east pediment of the Parthenon – reclining, headless torsos with elegant, marble folds and curves, and a single, expressive horse's head draped over the edge of its plinth.

Vlak, though, had stopped short, just before the shallow steps, where a simple glass case stood on a black marble block. There was a low rope, about eighteen inches out from the base of the plinth, to keep visitors back from the case itself.

"'The Elgin Bands,'" read Jed, from an adjacent information panel. "'Twin gold bracelets with onyx (?) insets, discovered at the site of the Parthenon and removed at the same time as the sculptures in this gallery. Provenance and usage disputed. A possible gift to the goddess Athena, as recorded by the Treasurers of Athena (434 BC).'"

Vlak stared at the bracelets closely – each held upright by clear, acrylic clasps that allowed visitors to circle the case and see them from all sides. She stooped to look at the internal surfaces, where faint hieroglyphs were visible to a keen eye. As he moved round with her, Hutch could see a glint from the polished stone that an alien had told him definitely weren't onyx insets on things that definitely weren't bracelets. Or at least not the sort of bracelets that the British Museum thought they were.

"Vlak?"

She looked up with a start. "Yes, it's them," she said.

"You're sure?" Jed had moved to her side and was looking intently at them.

"Those are the devices, I'm certain."

Sully was casting his eyes around the rest of the gallery. There were still quite a few visitors coming and going, including people walking right past them on their way for a closer look at the pediment sculptures.

"Any ideas?" he said. Jed's smash-and-grab was still the only suggestion on the table, but looking around, he didn't see how that was going to work. He doubted the glass in the case was actually glass – or if it was, that it would break easily. And with all these people around, how far would any of them get?

"I need to place a device on my arm for it to work," said Vlak, as two more visitors passed by.

"Keep your voice down!" said Hutch, hissing through clenched teeth. "We're normal tourists, remember, looking at the lovely bracelets."

"We need to be here when there are fewer people around," said Jed. "When the museum, opens, maybe, so we're the first in? Then create a distraction, something like that."

"Still don't see how we're going to get them out of there, let Vlak do her thing, and then get out ourselves, without getting nabbed," whispered Sully. "There must be security cameras everywhere. And what about him?"

Sully nodded his head at a seated gallery attendant in the corner, twenty feet away. He might be staring idly into the mid-distance now, wondering how long it was before closing time, and what he was going to have for dinner, but the sound of breaking glass in a museum tended to wake up the doziest of attendants.

"Dammit, we're so close!" said Jed. "Vlak, what do you think?"

She turned to look at them. "What would happen to you all, if I take the devices and go home? If they catch you?"

"When they catch us," said Sully. "I mean, realistically."

"Prison, probably. I mean, these are the freakin' Elgin Bands! It's not like we're stealing stuff from the gift shop," said Hutch.

"Prison, if we're lucky," said Jed. "The scary men in shades figure out we're here and doing this, and we'll be in a black-site interrogation facility before you know it. They won't be happy we helped an alien escape. They've got lots of special ways to show their unhappiness. There's a guy on YouTube with extra-long legs says he was hung upside down for a year in a cell."

"Then," said Vlak, "we need a better idea. Jed's right, there are too many others here."

"Back to the flat?" said Sully. "Get some sleep, figure out a plan for tomorrow morning?"

"And hope we're still not on anyone's radar by then," said Hutch.

Vlak turned back to the display case. She seemed understandably reluctant to leave, and Jed didn't blame her. On the run for, what, four days now? And so, so close, after the initial shock of thinking that there was no way off the planet. Here it was – her escape route, a couple of feet away in a glass case.

He watched her place one foot over the barrier rope, as she leaned forward for a closer look at the bracelets.

"We better go, Vlak," he said, tapping her elbow, as she put her hand out to the case. He could hardly blame her – he desperately wanted to touch them himself. Contact with an alien artefact! If this was how he felt, he couldn't imagine what she was feeling.

There was a loud cough from over in the corner, as the attendant finally noticed them.

"Stand behind the rope, please, madam," he said loudly, as he rose from his chair.

"Vlak!" Jed pulled at her elbow, as both Sully and Hutch turned to apologise to the attendant.

"Come on!" said Hutch. Then, in a lower, urgent voice, "We really don't want to be making a scene."

Vlak stepped back, as the others apologised again for her. Jed grabbed her wrist to go, but felt a pulsing sensation. Her smart-help had lit up and he could see a sequence of pin-prick lights flashing on the screen. Vlak glanced at her wrist and then looked back at the display case.

The attendant had started walking towards them and was perhaps ten feet away, checking his watch. His view of the case was blocked by Sully and Hutch, with Jed and Vlak behind them, just by the barrier rope.

Another couple of steps and he would be able to

see what Vlak could see – Jed, too, once he had followed the line of her eyes.

On the internal surfaces of the two bracelets, the faint hieroglyphs were flashing in unison, while the dark onyx bands had brightened to an amber glow.

Chapter 45

Jed pulled Vlak away as the attendant reached the display case, and they stood together with Hutch and Sully.

"The museum will be closing shortly," said the attendant. He had his back to the bracelets – Jed could still see the flashes as the hieroglyphs continued to pulse.

Vlak put her arm behind her back to hide her smart-help, which now also had a matching sequence of lights running across its face. Jed could see that Hutch had noticed the bracelets, too, as a glow lit up the display case.

"We're just leaving," said Jed. "Sorry, you know, about – " and then he stopped, realising he was drawing attention to the one thing he really didn't want the attendant to turn round and look at. He and Vlak stepped further back, followed by Hutch and Sully.

"That's all right, we just prefer it if you stay behind

the barrier," said the attendant. "Can't be too careful." He winked at Vlak. "They're pretty valuable, you know."

He turned slightly towards the display case, as Vlak took several decisive steps away, towards the gallery exit.

"Two and a half thousand years old," said the attendant. "I always think they look like they were made yesterday. Quite remarkable, really."

He looked straight at the bracelets, almost lovingly. "I always ask for this gallery, it's my favourite one in the whole museum."

The bracelets stood proud on their display stands inside the case – twin gold circles, each with an onyx inset, looking as bright and vibrant as they day they were unearthed in the rubble of the Parthenon. Faint hieroglyphs on the internal bands, just about visible to a keen eye.

No lights, no flashing, nothing untoward.

Jed breathed a huge sigh of relief and turned with Vlak for the exit, followed by the other two. She showed Jed her arm as they walked – her smart-help had also returned to its usual inert state.

Back in the Great Court, they collapsed on a bench – part of the café seating that was laid out in this section. There was a 'Sorry, Closed' notice on the long counter, with staff coming and going from behind a high, raised screen that ran its length.

"What the heck, Vlak?"

"Is there anything you do that isn't going to give me a heart attack?"

"Proximity alert," she said. "They pair, when able, with a help. I didn't think they would be that sensitive."

"It would have been all over, if he'd seen that," said Sully.

"Perhaps," said Vlak. "Although they go back into rest mode once there's sufficient distance, as you saw. They're designed to be unobtrusive. Or else they would have been identified by now."

"They're real, then," Hutch said, matter-of-factly.

"Of course they're real," said Jed.

In truth, Hutch hadn't thought there was any 'of course' about it. His view of what was real or not had been thoroughly scrambled.

Could he explain what had happened over the last few days, unless Vlak really was an alien? No, he couldn't.

Did he think that those two gold bracelets, displayed in a gallery in the British Museum, were some sort of alien transportation device? No, deep down, not really. They looked like ancient bracelets – no different to hundreds, probably thousands, of others that the museum had in cases all over the building.

At least, until they started flashing when an alien got within a couple of feet of them.

"It's a good thing, really," said Vlak. "They haven't been activated since they were first left on the planet, and they could have been damaged at any point in the meantime. But they seem to be working."

Café staff were cleaning up around them, stacking cups and plates on trays and then disappearing behind the counter and screen.

"It's ten past eight," said Hutch. "They're going to chuck us out soon. The museum opens again at ten tomorrow morning."

"If that's the security," said Sully, "just one bloke in the gallery, maybe we can come back first thing tomorrow and distract him? One of us could pretend to have a stroke or something. That shouldn't be hard. I feel like I've had about three today already."

Hutch knew it wouldn't be that simple. "That's not going to be the only security, is it?" he said. "What about cameras, CCTV? Then we've still got to break into the case, and get the bracelets. How long's all that going to take? How are we going to get away with it? Once the doors open, there'll be people coming in. Even if we're first, that won't give us much time. How long do we need, anyway?"

"Vlak?"

"The devices will pair as I approach, you've seen that. I need to put one on my wrist for it to work. There's a sequence to run on the smart-help, and a similar sequence on the device itself. It will take two minutes before I'm ready to travel."

"And then we're left standing next to an empty case, trying to pretend it was nothing to do with us. Plus, the attendant is bound to remember he'd already seen us hanging around the day before."

A café assistant sprayed and wiped the table next to them, and gave them a pointed look. Time to go.

"Unless," said Jed, beckoning them all to their feet, away from the table. They joined a handful of late stragglers still in the Great Court, while a final tour group headed past them for the exit, behind a guide holding a little flag.

"Mysterious one you are," said Sully in a Yoda voice. "Cunning plan you have?"

"Unless we do a *Night at the Museum* job," said Jed. "Ben Stiller the shit out of this place."

"Yeah, right," said Hutch. "Come on, let's go. We've got a lot to think about."

"I'm serious," said Jed. "It's perfect. We hide until everyone's gone, and then we've got the place to ourselves, all the time we need."

"Hide? Where?"

They looked around the sweeping Great Court, fast emptying of visitors. On the opposite side of the vast space, the information desk had already closed. Closer to them, at the base of the central rotunda, uniformed staff were pulling the shutters down over the racks and stalls of the museum shop. A tannoy announcement repeated that the museum would be closing to the public in five minutes.

"Now would be the time to reveal your cunning plan," said Sully.

"I hadn't really got beyond 'locking ourselves in the British Museum,'" said Jed. "I'm thinking."

A couple of gallery attendants sauntered past the

café and exchanged a few words with the staff, who were finishing off the cleaning. There was some laughter and then the attendants walked on. "Exit's that way, guys," they called, as they passed.

Jed had dropped to his knees, pretending to tie his shoelaces to buy some time.

"Come on, let's go, this is hopeless," said Hutch.

"No, wait." Jed pointed, as the last two café assistants emerged from behind the high screen at the back of the counter, carrying coats and bags. They walked off chatting, not looking back, and Jed waited until they were twenty or thirty feet away before darting across. He beckoned furiously and the others followed, then they all slipped behind the screen.

The front of the screen, facing the Great Court, had the café menu printed on it, and was hung with display racks for snacks and drinks. The screen was about twelve feet high and thirty feet across, running the length of the counter that stood in front of it.

Behind – where they were now standing – was the service area for the café. There was a double sink, a preparation bench, a row of recycling bins, and a long line of deep cupboards, the height of the screen, all closed.

"Genius," said Hutch. "This doesn't look suspicious at all. Hiding by the bins."

They could hear footsteps out in the Great Court, as more final visitors and staff made their way towards the main exit.

Jed pushed at one of the cupboard doors and the

latch sprung. The door opened. Four feet deep, eight feet wide, twelve feet high – and mercifully empty apart from a couple of boxes of crisps and chocolate bars in one corner.

"Bloody Houdini's done it again."

"You're welcome," said Jed. "Quick, get in, all of you."

Chapter 46

They stood side by side, in the dark, in silence, for what seemed like an eternity. Eventually, Jed cracked the door open a little and listened. They hadn't heard anything close by for a while, but it was a huge museum and there were distant bangs and clanks that could have been cleaners starting work.

"We can't stay in here," said Sully. "I mean, brilliant idea, don't get me wrong, where would we be without you, but this is a bloody store cupboard in the bloody British Museum. It's not your best work, Jed."

They extricated themselves and kept out of sight behind the screen while they pondered their next move.

"God, we're actually going to do it?" said Hutch. "Actually steal some gold bracelets?"

"Not steal," said Vlak. "If they belong to anyone on this planet, they belong to me."

"Let's hope we don't have to try and explain that to anyone."

"According to you, everything in here has been stolen from someone else anyway," said Sully.

"This seems like the best time to you, to have a discussion about imperialism?"

"Just saying, Trotsky, that Vlak's right. They're hers if they're anyone's."

"I'm sure the judge will take that into consideration, before – "

"Will you both shut the hell up," hissed Jed. "We need to move. Any ideas?"

"We need somewhere better than a snack cupboard to hide out, at least until the cleaners have done their rounds."

"I'm having some crisps, though," said Jed. He stashed a few packets away and then, feeling guilty, found a fiver in his pocket and left it on top of one of the boxes.

"We can't just stroll around the museum," said Hutch. "What about security cameras? They must be all over the place?"

He looked up at the high walls of the Great Court behind the café screen. There were no obvious mounted cameras here, but when he peered around the edge of the screen, across the large expanse, he could see tell-tale grey boxes set high on ledges, trained on the gallery entrances. More, undoubtedly, lay in wait further inside the museum.

"Great. So, we're stuck in the crisp cupboard?" said Sully. "Nice one, Jed."

Vlak tapped her smart-help, held her arm above

her head and rotated it back and forth a few times. Then she brought her arm back down and touched another button, and a holographic image popped up – a 3D floor plan with black pulsing dots marked at intervals.

"Security cameras," she said. "Although it's a generous use of the word 'security.' This seems to be a very primitive system based solely on visual imaging."

"So, what? You can zap them all, or something?"

"You're very keen on zapping things. It seems to be a planetary obsession. No, I can't control them from here. But I know where to go, if we do want to disable them." Vlak pinched the image, and lines from each of the pulsing black dots – the CCTV cameras – converged on a single point on the floor plan.

"What's that?"

"The control centre, I imagine," said Vlak. She passed her hand over the hologram and the image flattened out to show the location where all the lines met. "Behind us, in the entrance lobby," she pointed. "Down the corridor a little way, there's a room on the left."

"Where we'll find what?" said Hutch.

"Probably a bored little man in front of a big bank of monitors," said Sully. "Right?"

"I have no information," said Vlak. "But that's where we should go first, if we want to avoid detection."

"Won't someone see us coming?"

"Possibly," said Vlak. "But it won't matter. If there's anyone in there, I can – help them forget. Like before."

They listened silently for a full minute, waiting to see if they could hear anyone approaching, and then – one by one – slipped out from behind the screen and dashed for the museum's main entrance. They regrouped close to the wall, and followed Vlak down the corridor on tiptoes, nerves taut, waiting for a shout from a passing attendant or cleaner.

Outside a door that said, 'Private, Authorised Staff Only,' Hutch raised a finger to his lips and they retreated a few paces, and whispered among themselves.

"We'll all have to go in. We can't stay here, we're right out in the open."

"If there's anyone in there, they're going to freak."

"Can't be helped. You just need to get to them first, right, Vlak? You've got a plan?"

She nodded and they moved towards the door. "And this plan does not involve hitting anyone, OK?" said Hutch to Jed.

Vlak tried the handle and the door swung open. A security guard sat at a desk, with his back to them, with two TV screens showing scrolling images of museum corridors and exhibition spaces. There was an opened tube of Pringles on the desk, a coffee cup next to it, and a side table with a kettle on.

At the sound of the door, the guard turned. "Didn't expect you so soon, mate, I thought – " He stopped when he saw Vlak advance through the door. The others had held back, unseen for the moment.

"Hello?" He looked confused. "What are you doing

here, miss? You shouldn't be in here. Staff exit's the other way. Back down the corridor."

Vlak came further into the room. "Are you the little man?" she said.

From behind her, out in the corridor, came a muffled, exasperated, "Fuck's sake."

"What?" The guard looked more closely at Vlak. T-shirt, denim jacket, bucket hat scrunched up and sticking out of one of the pockets. She didn't look much like any of the smartly dressed young people who staffed the information desks in the museum.

"What are you doing here?" he said. "Are you new or something?"

"I would like to hold your hand," said Vlak. "Just for a moment."

"What?" Now he really looked perturbed, and rose from his seat. "What did you say?"

"It only works if I can create a firm skin-to-skin seal." Vlak moved closer and held out her hands. "Please," she said, beckoning.

"Now hang on, miss." The guard stood tall. "I don't know what you think – "

"Oh, for fuck's sake," said Sully, moving into the room, followed by Hutch and Jed, who closed the door behind them. "This was your plan?"

The guard looked wildly from one to the other, lost momentarily for words.

"I thought a simple, clear explanation would be best," said Vlak.

"Unbelievable. Couldn't you have, I don't know,

fluttered your eyelashes at him a bit? Used your feminine wiles?"

"Pretended to be a human female?"

"Yes! Anything, except, you know, tell him what you were going to do. Flash him some skin, wink at him, whatever."

"And this would work as a distraction?" said Vlak. "Interesting. You are a very odd species." She tried a stage wink at the guard, who recoiled.

"Who the hell are you lot?" he said, reaching for a walkie-talkie on his desk.

"Now then, chief, we don't want to do that," said Jed, grabbing it first. "Let Vlak here have a little feel of your hand and then we can all go about our business."

"Is this a sex thing?" said the guard. "I mean, her, fair enough. You – " he nodded at Sully – "maybe. But you – " he gestured at Jed and shook his head.

"Rude. Wish I did have my selfie stick now."

The guard had taken his eyes off Vlak, which gave her the opportunity she needed. She leaned forward and grabbed one of his wrists, and looked straight into his eyes as he turned in alarm.

"Hey!"

"Just listen to my voice," she said. His eyes glazed slightly and his stance softened, as Vlak helped him back into his chair.

"Well, that nearly went tits-up," said Hutch. "Excellent job, everyone. Top bit of planning."

"If you had explained earlier about using my body,"

said Vlak, "I see now that it might have been better. Tits-up, yes?"

"Can we just concentrate on mind-melding this horny sod and get out of here?"

Vlak held onto the guard's wrist and continued speaking as she looked into his eyes. "We were never here," she said. "This has just been a normal evening. You fell asleep for a while."

"Normal," muttered the guard. "Asleep."

She turned her attention to the monitors, spending a minute cross-checking the hologram image on her smart-help with the scrolling images from the camera feeds.

"Which is the way to the gallery with the devices?" she said.

Hutch plotted it out for her on the map projected from her smart-help, and Vlak touched each individual black dot en route that represented a security camera. Images flashed on the screens as she did it, and then she turned back to the guard, looking satisfied.

"All done? Actually, what *have* you done?"

"The relays will just display the current views, synced to my help. Anyone looking will see what can be seen now – which is nothing. When I leave – " and here, Vlak pointed up into the air – "the system will crash and the images won't be able to be retrieved."

"And him?"

"He won't remember anything. He'll come round soon and as far as he's concerned, everything will be working perfectly."

Vlak turned the guard back to face the desk and settled him in his seat. He slumped a little and burbled.

They turned for the door, but Jed held back, obviously still smarting. "Rude git. Vlak, tell him he didn't bring any Pringles to work today."

He leaned across and picked up the tube. "Right, come on then, let's see if the camera-zappy business worked."

Chapter 47

Back at the entrance to the Great Court, they peered carefully around the pillars at the edge.

On this side of the central rotunda, at least, it was deserted – they could hear faint noises off in the distance, but the way through to the portico and museum galleries beyond was clear. It was also very open, with no place to hide. Hundreds of feet of space before the portico, and no real way of knowing what lay beyond.

"Cameras didn't show anyone down there, right?"

"As far as we could see. But who knows if they have every angle covered."

There was nothing for it but to go. Sully went first, padding silently across the limestone floor and then speeding up the closer he got to the doorway. Vlak next, then Jed and Hutch together – and they all caught their breath, flattened against the huge pillars of the portico.

Beyond, it was a straight shot back down to the Parthenon Gallery, but it meant crossing through the middle of exhibition galleries on both sides. They started to creep forward, keeping low, using display cases and enormous statues as cover, and ran out of luck almost immediately. As they hovered at the threshold to the next room, someone turned a corner in a distant gallery, their footsteps echoing ever closer.

"Now what?"

"One each!" Hutch whispered and pointed, and they hunkered down behind the plinths of four life-sized marble statues that lined one side of the room. The footsteps got louder and closer and were then in the room itself, passing the first two statues, where Vlak and Jed were shifting silently to keep out of sight.

As the security guard passed, Jed could see the back of him – and willed him to keep moving. At which point, the guard promptly stopped to answer a squawk from his walkie-talkie.

Hutch and Sully were now directly to his left, each hidden behind a plinth, squeezing in their shoulders and thighs. Sweat dripped off the end of Hutch's nose – he could almost believe it made a sound as it dropped to the floor, and he closed his eyes tight and held his breath.

"On my way, mate," said the guard, "stick the kettle on." There was an answering squawk, to which the guard replied, "No, I haven't got your bloody Pringles." And then he hitched up his belt and moved on, the sound of his footsteps receding into the distance as he headed out towards the Great Court.

They watched him turn the corner and then slipped out from behind the statues, moving quickly into the next room, where they stood flat against the wall, out of the line of sight. Hutch tried to bring his heart rate down, breathing out quietly through pursed lips.

This room had stone friezes and some low sculptures – the Parthenon Gallery was straight ahead. Nowhere obvious to hide in either place.

"This isn't as much fun as in the movies," said Sully. "We might have dealt with the cameras, but we can't keep hiding behind statues all night." He looked across at a crouching stone lion. "And one of them better not move or talk to me."

"There," said Hutch, who had been casting around for inspiration.

On the righthand side of the room, at the far end, was a reconstructed monumental tomb, more than twenty feet high. A wall of decorated marble blocks formed a rectangle, reaching above head height, topped by columns and statues that sat under a sculpted roof.

Sully boosted Vlak up first and then Hutch, both wedging toes in the cracked marble blocks and squeezing between the columns and the statues. Jed followed, kicking against the marble relief sculptures as he went, and then they reached down and pulled up Sully, before dropping into the relative safety of the interior.

"This is pretty cool," grinned Jed. He kept his voice low as he checked everyone was all right. "Coming up for ten o'clock," he said, looking at his phone. "We should give it a couple of hours at least, right?"

"See how often they come down this way," agreed Hutch. "The bracelets are next door, but once we're in there, there's no hiding place. We're only going to get one shot at it."

"But look at this place," said Sully. He gestured at the foursquare walls, where they were completely hidden from sight. He was beginning to see a way out of this after all.

If they could get the bracelets out of the display case quickly – if Vlak could get them to work – if no one saw them – if they could get back to the sanctuary of this hiding place afterwards – then they might just be able to sneak out the next morning under cover of the museum's first visitors.

"That's a lot of ifs," said Hutch. But he agreed, it was the best chance they had. Probably the only chance to get away without being caught.

"Where are we anyway?" said Sully. "What are we desecrating?"

Jed brought up a museum floor plan on his phone. "The Nereid Monument," he said. "Tomb of King Arbinas. Two thousand four hundred years old. I think I chipped a bit off the side as I came up. You know, I could probably – "

He stopped talking as Hutch raised his finger,

urgently, and jabbed it up and outwards. Listening intently, they could hear a low-pitched droning noise and then a sort of scuffling sound at the far end of the room.

The machine noise ebbed and flowed as it worked its way up and down the length of the gallery, at one point circling right around the base of the monument. A tuneless voice sang a few lines from a song and then broke into some terribly mis-timed rapping. Then machine and operator were off into the Parthenon Gallery beyond, before passing through again on their way back towards the Great Court.

"That's the cleaners then," said Hutch, once silence fell again. "Bloody Ed Sheeran? This is not going to be restful, is it?"

"Let's wait and see if there's another circuit by the security guy. At least that should tell us how long we might have in there without interruption."

"So, this is our plan, is it?" said Sully. "Wait in this creepy old tomb for an hour or two? I mean, I'm not complaining, it's better than Vlak's plan with the randy warder, and it's better than the snack cupboard."

"Unless you've got a better idea," said Jed, settling back against a marble block. He distributed Pringles and crisps. "Vlak, you OK? Happy to wait a bit longer?"

"It's fine, Jed. Can I have one of the curved potatoes, please?"

"There you go then. Nothing to do now except

wait," said Jed. "I'm having the prawn cocktail crisps, I paid for them."

Which is when the 'Crazy Frog' ringtone from Sully's phone started to echo off the internal walls of the ancient tomb of a long-dead Lycian king.

Chapter 48

UK Border Force
Re: Passport trace request, France-UK Border Control

'URGENT. The US diplomatic passport you enquired about [Mr. Brock Anderson, other details supplied] was used to enter the UK at a Eurostar crossing (Brussels–London) earlier today at 14.42.

We're still waiting on video confirmation from the cameras at the control point, but thought you would appreciate the heads-up at the earliest opportunity.'

Voice note, to: Head of Operations, BEVI Research Unit
From: X-Team agent, Athens, Greece

'Prof, you've seen the wire? That's Matey. I think we've been played. The American special-ops gun was found

The Wrong Stop

in Brussels, and then the passport was used to get someone into the UK – no video yet from passport control, but we do have this CCTV from St Pancras station, which you'll find very interesting.

[*Video attached*] Tell me that's not Pocket Guy? The US agent ID'd him in Berlin, and we spotted him getting on the Brussels train – put a cap and a jacket on him, change the angle, what do you reckon? That was him in Prague, too, surely?

So, we're saying Matey's in London? Or he was eight hours ago. Meantime, we're strung out all over Europe, waiting for him to turn up here in Athens. But it looks like he's done the old switcheroo. Tricky little blighter, I'll say that for him.

Anyway, I've scrambled the team – all systems go for London.'

Chapter 49

"You left your ringer on? You idiot!"

"I thought I'd turned it off." Sully jabbed at his phone in panic, trying to mute the sound. They all grimaced and froze, listening for the tell-tale footsteps of a security guard lumbering down the halls of the museum, curious to see who was phoning King Arbinas.

They waited for a few seconds, but heard nothing, except a wavering voice from the phone saying, "Neil?", repeatedly.

"You answered it as well, you moron!"

"I didn't mean to." Sully looked stricken and checked the screen.

"Who is it?"

"God, it's my mum."

"You've got to be kidding. Hang up!"

"I can't, she'll just keep ringing back. You don't

know what she's like. I said I'd call her when we got back. I forgot all about it."

"Christ, get rid of her then. Quickly."

Sully leaned into his phone and whispered. "Hi Mum."

"Oh, thank goodness, Neil. I wondered what was going on. I thought you were going to call when you got back? I know it's late, but I just wanted to check that you were all right – "

"Mum, it's not really a good time. Can I call you back?"

"Honestly, Neil, I haven't heard anything from you for three weeks. Anything could have happened. I know what it's like abroad. Your Auntie Nell once brought a box of biscuits home from Brittany and it had a spider in it."

Sully closed his eyes, muttered "God, here we go," and then said, "Mum, seriously, It's only Europe. I've been away with Hutch and Jed, on holiday – "

"Oh, yes, how lovely. Hutch, such a nice boy. Now, remind me, is Jed the one who plays with the little painted soldiers?"

"Orcs," hissed Jed. "Honestly. Green, with pointy ears, how are they soldiers?"

"Look, Mum, I really can't – "

"Well, your father wants to know when you're coming down to see us, because he'd quite like to choose a nice new colour for your bedroom. Now I told him you wouldn't mind what colour it was, but you know what your father … "

"Mum – "

" ... and B&Q have got some quite lovely colours, only I told your father, it still has to look nice for Neil, for when he brings back his friends ... "

Sully held out his phone as his mother continued talking, and mouthed to the others, "Unbelievable."

"Anyway, dear, I'm glad you've had a lovely holiday. Although a postcard would have been nice."

"Postcard, sure. Sorry about that. Look, Mum, something's come up, I'll call you tomorrow, promise."

Sully cut the call and sat back, shaking his head.

"Jesus."

"Yes, Neil, that's very naughty, a postcard would have been lovely," said Hutch.

"That was your mum?" said Vlak.

"Are you sure you want Daddy to paint over the nice unicorns, though," said Jed.

"Jed, have you also exchanged lips and tongues with Sully's mum?" said Vlak. "She does sound very nice. And lovely."

"Sod off, the lot of you," said Sully.

"For the record, I have not snogged anyone's mum," said Jed.

"Have you got a mum, Vlak? She'll want to be careful around Jed."

"How did this become about me?" Jed looked indignant. "I'm not the moron who left his phone on in a stake-out in a tomb."

They all looked at each other and dissolved into dry,

heaving laughter, shushing each other as it threatened to get out of control.

"It is a nice, lovely tomb," said Vlak, to more snorts.

"You can sod off, as well. Is it nearly time for you to go?" said Sully.

Jed checked his watch. "Ten," he said. "We should do it as close to opening as we dare. Less time for anyone to discover the bracelets are gone. So that means spending the night in here. The next few hours, anyway."

"Nice," said Hutch, to a punch in the arm from Sully.

They stretched out at the foot of the tomb as best they could, Hutch next to Sully on one flank, Jed and Vlak on the other.

"Have you got a mum, though, Vlak?" asked Jed. He'd been wondering about the very many things that still seemed to be unanswered about the single most interesting person he'd ever met.

"Not really," she said. "It's – "

"Complicated, sure. It's just, I don't really understand anything about your life, your world. Where you come from, what it's like."

"It's very hard to explain. We – experience. We – simply are. Our relationships are – many. And one."

"OK. Very clear."

"I told you, it's hard to explain. You have to experience it to understand it. Our minds are entwined in ways that yours are not. It's – encompassing, protective, nurturing. Perhaps like the relationships you have with your mothers, although those appear to be individual and my world is a – plurality."

"I wouldn't know," said Jed. "I don't have a mum."

Sully heard the exchange and looked up. "I didn't know that. How come?"

"You just assumed I did. You never asked," said Jed. "She died. A long time ago."

"Shit, man, I'm sorry. I'd never have made those jokes if I'd have known. What about your dad?"

"Waste of space. Never painted my bedroom, that's for sure." He smiled ruefully at Sully.

"Jed, man, that's – "

"Nothing, is what it is. Don't worry about it."

There was a slight, awkward silence, and then they settled back against the marble blocks.

"What are you going to do, when all this is over?" said Jed.

"What, if we manage to stay out of prison?" said Hutch.

"Let's pretend."

"Well, for one, I'm never going on holiday with Sully again. Or speaking to strangers on a train. No offence."

"Yeah, well I'm sticking with the rugger boys from now on. I could have been in Ayia Napa, all this time, instead of hiding out in a museum. A bloody museum! Managed to spend an entire year in London without going into one, until tonight."

"Back to college, then?" said Jed.

"Sure, back to college. What else are we going to do?"

"After all this," said Jed. "You think we can just go back. Knowing what we know?" He gestured at Vlak.

"What do we know?" said Sully. "She's going to bugger off home. And good luck to you, don't get me wrong. But it's not like *we've* been granted superpowers or anything. We don't get to keep any of the fancy tech. Life's not going to change for us."

"I apologise, Sully." Vlak looked at him, seriously. "I didn't realise you wanted superpowers. You should have said. Which ones would you like?"

"You're pretty funny, for an alien."

"I've had excellent teachers. I will miss this – hanging out?"

"You don't hang with friends?"

"It's not really like that, where I come from. We are all connected, equally. The bonds between us are all the same."

"Sounds a barrel of laughs, your planet."

"It's just different. You can't think that, across the entire expanse of the universe, the only way of doing things is the one you experience, here on this planet? Anyway, we have jokes."

"Go on."

"How many Earthlings does it take to change a diode in a ship's surge protector?"

"I don't know, how many?"

"Only one, if you insert the probe correctly."

Chapter 50

Email from Department of History, King's College, London
To: Prof. James Storm
From: Dr. Marcus Stewart
Subject: Intriguing assignment!

Hi Jim,

I can't even begin to guess what this is about – but, I know, national security and all that. You have the best job! And yes, I also know, if you told me, you'd have to kill me…

Sorry, it's taken me a while to get onto this, by the way. Term starts again soon and I'm up to my eyes in course prep.

Anyway, I had a look at the historical record, within the parameters you gave me – pretty bloody wide, by the way. Got some keen grad students to do the donkey work, they're used to getting bizarre requests like this from me, don't worry.

The Wrong Stop

Most of the stuff we can discount – we've got corroborative evidence from other sources and records. Meteorological, atmospheric, geological, you name it. We can explain most of the phenomena.

But there is one that fits the profile. 'Lights in the sky – unusual sounds – angry gods,' that sort of thing. There are a couple of clear references from contemporary sources in the historical record, dated 434 BC, which we can't then fix to a recorded or inferred natural phenomenon.

As for location, the contemporary reports said it was visible over Athens, as you had suggested.

Then we zeroed in on the Parthenon and checked the Treasury records. There's a whole history here I won't bore you with, but basically there's what we academics like to call a shitload of hard evidence – literally, carved on marble tablets.

Again, it's difficult to be certain about anything, given that you can't tell me – or you don't know – exactly what it is I'm looking for! But the Treasury records are incredibly detailed – names, nationalities, ranks, dates, amounts, that sort of thing.

In the time frame you gave me, there are three 'gifts' or donations that the Treasurers recorded that are simply ascribed to a 'Stranger' or 'Foreigner.' That could be someone from anywhere that wasn't greater ancient Greece – sorry, I can't be more specific, unless you have more info to share.

I've attached all the research, anyway. Make of it what you will.

One of the 'gifts,' by the way, is thought to be the 'Elgin Bands' – you know, the gold bracelets in the British Museum? Not that there's any real evidence linking the Treasurers' record with the specific gift, but it's a neat coincidence.

Is that any help?

Hope so. Let's get a beer sometime?

Marcus

Chapter 51

Hutch woke up with a crick in his neck. He stretched his legs and checked his phone. Six am.

He had no idea how he – any of them – had managed to sleep at all, on the stone floor of an ancient tomb. They had heard one other guard doing his rounds, three hours ago now, but they had stopped short of the room they were in, and no one else had walked on through to the Parthenon Gallery.

He woke the rest of them up carefully, so that no one made any unnecessary noise. They had all double-checked their phones were on silent since Sully's unplanned chat with his mum.

"What do you think?" he said, as the others stirred. "Time to do it?"

"As good a time as any," said Sully. "You ready to go home, Vlak?"

"Yes, thank you, Sully. It's time." She checked her

smart-help. Still inert, though once they approached the bracelets, they knew it would fire up again.

"We're all going, right?" said Hutch. "We'll need a look-out at the gallery entrance. Two of us to try and lift the glass case off, while Vlak does her stuff?"

"Then straight back here, dive in with the dead guy again until the museum opens. Got it."

"You know he's not actually in here? The king?"

"I'm sticking with my version, makes a better story," said Sully.

"You know you can't tell anyone? Ever?"

"Oh, bollocks," said Jed. "Bollocks, bollocks, bollocks." He rocked on his knees.

"All right, big guy. We're all aching, calm down."

"It's not that." Jed turned his phone so that they could see. "I set up a Google alert for any more news about Vlak. Or at least, anything else about that photo they were showing in Berlin. Anything to do with 'man-hunt,' that sort of thing."

"And?"

"There's another photo," said Jed. He scrolled and touched his screen, and showed them.

"Oh, right – "

"Don't tell me that's *you*?"

On a news story where the biggest word they could see was 'Wanted,' was quite a clear image of Jed, travelling down the escalators at the station in Berlin. There was another of him standing alone in the arrivals space at St Pancras station.

"It is you. What do they want you for?"

The final photo was of two juxtaposed images. The original one of Vlak, captured at Prague's station from on high, wearing her distinctive cap and jacket. And, next to it, one of Jed from a similar angle at St Pancras. Similar height, similar pose. Face obscured in both. One with a cap and jacket, one without.

"Christ, they think you're Vlak!"

"They're going to be very disappointed when they catch you," said Sully. "Cross, too, probably, when they find out they've just chased a gamer-nerd all over Europe, instead of an alien."

"It's not funny"

"It kind of is. And, in fact, this is good."

"How is this any kind of good? My photo is being plastered all over the internet?"

"Yeah, but it means they're not looking for Vlak. I mean, they are, but now they've got you mixed up, they're after you instead. If the bracelets work, they'll never even know she was here."

"That's good news for Vlak," said Hutch. "Probably. But when they catch Captain Astro-Pocket here – and they definitely will – it won't take much probing to discover he's no alien."

"I can't be probed," said Jed. "I have a very low tolerance for pain. I'd give you two up in a heartbeat."

"But they're your friends," said Vlak. "I understand that to be a special bond? You mean that you wouldn't suffer for their sake?"

"No, I bloody would not. First sign of a stick with a camera on it and I'm telling them everything."

"You are a very interesting species," said Vlak.

"You can talk," said Jed, bristling.

"Look," said Hutch, "as things stand, none of this changes anything. Are we helping Vlak or not?"

"Suppose."

"Good, let's worry about one thing at a time. There are still a million ways all this can go wrong, and then it won't just be you with your face all over the TV."

They climbed quietly out of the tomb and slipped across to the entrance to the Parthenon Gallery. Two, tall glass doors blocked their way, but they opened with a slight creak that echoed down the halls. They padded quickly through, past the side galleries, and moved into the main display hall, ducking around the corner to stay out of sight of any roaming guard.

Fifty feet away, at the far end, stood the glass case holding the Elgin Bands. They moved forward together in a line, Vlak advancing with her arm held out before her.

"That thing better not have a ring tone," said Hutch, under his breath.

Ten feet from the case, the screen on Vlak's smart-help brightened, and once they were almost within touching distance they could see the pattern of pin-prick lights from the bracelets, just as before.

"They're primed," said Vlak. "But we have to get them out of the case."

"Easier said than done." Hutch laid his hands tentatively on the glass. "How do we know this thing won't set off an alarm, the minute we try to open it?"

"It won't," said Vlak. She scanned her smart-help around all four sides of the case and around the lower plinth. "No system detected."

"Don't suppose that thing's got a handy laser beam attachment, then?" said Hutch. He shook the case slightly, and then ran his hands down to stop at the stainless-steel locks that fixed the glass case to the plinth, one on each side.

"Why does everyone think I've got a laser beam?" said Vlak. She bent down and put her hands on one of the locks, and joined with Hutch as they tried to wrench the case upwards. It didn't move.

"Stand back," said Jed, flourishing a red, contoured pocketknife. "I've got this." He unfolded a selection of blades and utensils, slid one under one of the locks and banged hard with the heel of his palm. There was a loud click and the case lifted very slightly off the plinth. "Told you," he said. "Pockets. You never know when you're going to need something. Swiss Army Knife, classic tool."

"You said it, mate,' said Sully, but Jed ignored him and carried on. With the others keeping an eye on the main entrance, Jed went to work on the remaining three sides, and then he and Vlak carefully lifted the glass case up and over the bracelets.

She stood right in front of them for the first time and lifted her hands close, palms up, without touching them. The onyx bands had turned a bright, glowing amber, while the lights on both the smart-help and the bracelets had synchronised into a rapid cycle of repeating patterns.

"Is this it?" said Hutch. "Is it happening?"

"Almost," said Vlak. "Once they're on my other wrist, there's only one more sequence to run. I only need one device, but I'm not leaving the other here to be found – they could be reverse-engineered to gain better access to my ship. And you're all going to need to stand back. The vortex is quite considerable."

"I don't even want to know what that means," said Hutch. "Well, I suppose this is goodbye?" He looked round at the other two. "Right? We need to get out of here."

"Not me," said Jed. He stepped forward, looked at the bracelets – still in their upright clasps – and then turned to the others. "I'm going with Vlak."

Chapter 52

Voice recording, Athens, Greece:

X-Team agent
- Yes, got it, he's going to the British Museum. I'm at the airport now.

Head of Operations, BEVI Research Unit
[response unavailable]

- Going to see his old Pharaoh mates, how would I know? Your college pal reckons it's something to do with the Acropolis and the Parthenon.

[response unavailable]

- I don't know what to think. They were here in ancient Greek times? Jesus, every wackjob on the internet is going to be flocking to Athens, if this ever gets out.

[response unavailable]

- I've got the crews on standby. Flight here leaves in an hour, arrives London, nine am local. Museum's open at ten, I'll be there.

[response unavailable]

- No, let's keep the museum open. Nothing out of the ordinary. We don't want to scare him off, now we've finally got an edge. We know where he's going, so we'll get in and hunker down. He sets foot through the door, we'll track and nab him, nice and easy.

[response unavailable]

- Alive and well, Prof, I know, that's the plan. Tap on the shoulder in a nice, quiet museum. But yeah, I know, slippery little bugger so far. If we have to trank him, we will.

[response unavailable]

- Hazmat suits, are you for real? I thought this was supposed to be a nice, quiet extraction?

[response unavailable]

- I never know if you're being serious. Acid for blood?

He better not get any on my trainers, they cost a fortune.

[response unavailable]

- Well, anything's possible. He could have just come to spread the word about universal peace and harmony. Have you thought about that?

[response unavailable]

- I suppose he did clunk that big American special-ops guy. Mind you, can hardly blame him. I find them really annoying and they're on my side. Well, humanity's side, I suppose.

[response unavailable]

- Look, gotta go, they're calling my flight. Don't worry, Prof. I'm going to bring you a nice, shiny alien and you can ask him all the questions you want.

Chapter 53

Hutch didn't quite believe what he had heard.

"You're doing what?"

"Going with her. You only need one, right, Vlak? That other one would work for me?"

Vlak had taken one of the bracelets off its stand. She held it next to her smart-help and the band cracked on one side of the onyx inset and opened. The hieroglyphs still danced with lights, as she pushed at an almost invisible indentation inside the circle, and then she slipped the bracelet on her other wrist and snapped it shut.

"It works for any organic being, Jed," she said.

"There you go then."

"That's not exactly a reason," said Hutch.

"He knows," said Jed, nodding at Sully. He reached forward and picked up the other bracelet.

"Jed's moving out of the flat," said Sully. "At least, I think so."

"You are?"

"I was going to tell you," said Jed. "It just never seemed to be the time."

"Hang on," said Hutch. "There's moving out and then there's – whatever this is. You're leaving the planet? You won't get your deposit back," he added, rather desperately.

"Solar system," said Vlak. "Not just the planet."

"Like that helps."

"I hate it," said Jed. "Not Earth, so much, though it mostly sucks, to be fair. College, though. I've been chucked out anyway. And every secret service in the world thinks I'm an alien. I might as well go."

"You don't hate it," said Hutch. "I mean, there's your dungeons and dragons, and you've got friends, and there's …" He trailed off, trying to think of what else Jed did have in his life.

"Not really, Hutch, let's be honest."

"You know we can't come and visit?" said Sully. "Student railcard doesn't cover intergalactic trips."

"You're taking this very well," said Hutch. "Tell him."

"Tell him what? He's got free will, a mind of his own," said Sully.

"Free will? Technically … " said Vlak. "Never mind, I'm not sure your species is ready for all that."

"You're not helping! Tell him he can't go. It's mad."

"Of course he can go, if he wants to. I think he'd like it. Jed is more open than you to the possibilities of this universe."

"That's because he believes any old shit!"

"You live on a small planet, in an inconsequential solar system, in a distant spiral of your galaxy," said Vlak. "Jed's friends in the videos say you haven't even gone to your local moon. You can't begin to imagine what's really out there. Not everything that seems impossible to you is untrue. Travel really does expand the mind – Jed will see it all, if he wants to."

"Look," said Sully. "We can stand about arguing until someone comes and finds us, or we can get on with this."

"I'm ready," said Jed.

"You're sure, mate?"

"Don't worry about me," said Jed. "It's the vortex you want to be worried about, right Vlak?"

He handed the second bracelet to her, and she held it next to her smart-help, so that it opened.

"What do those markings say anyway?" he said, as he took the bracelet back off her, the hieroglyphs still flashing in sequence. "It all looks very complicated."

"This one says, 'Press here,'" said Vlak, pointing at the indentation and pushing it. "The other bit says, 'Onlookers should stand well clear.'"

"You've got to be kidding. I thought it would be some kind of special incantation."

"I told you, they're for one-time emergency use. It's a simple push-and-go operation."

"To transport us out of the galaxy?"

"To the nearest wormhole interchange, yes. Don't worry, it's a standard jump."

Jed snapped the bracelet shut on his wrist. With Vlak's help, he then lifted the glass display case back onto the plinth. From a distance, it would look intact – it might buy the other two some time when the museum opened.

"Right then, boys. Don't wait up."

"You're seriously going?"

"Watch me. I kind of feel I've been waiting for this my whole life. I just didn't know it."

"We'll miss you," said Sully.

"No, you won't."

They looked at each other and smiled, ruefully.

"You're right, of course. What shall we do with your stuff?"

"Don't know, don't care. Actually, give the orcs to Josie in Mystery-Soc. And tell her I believe her, about Bigfoot."

"We will actually miss *you*," said Sully to Vlak. "It's been a blast." He reached forward and hugged her, followed by Hutch. "I mean, seriously, you couldn't have made it up. Well, Jed could, but you know what I mean."

"And I'll miss you both," said Vlak. "This has been most interesting. I didn't expect to make friends. I was most worried, if I'm honest, about the probing, but your planet has potential. I'm glad we met. I would never have found the devices without you – or had chips."

She touched a button on her smart-help and the sides rose as a hologram emerged – another schematic of lines and ellipses that dipped and whirled as she raised her arm. "Jed," she said. "Your device, the phone – you can't take it with you. The transporter won't recognise it. We don't want to trigger the failsafe auto-destruct."

"Christ, no, we don't," said Jed, handing his phone to Hutch, adding, "I'd get rid of the SIM card if I were you. The alien-hunters will be able to trace it."

"Until a few days ago, I'd have said you were bonkers, you know? Mind you, I think you still are." Hutch smiled at him.

"And I'd have said you had a closed mind, Hutch. But things change. Just get rid of the SIM."

Vlak finished her preparations. "You both need to stand clear," she said, "and don't look directly into the light. Ready?" she said to Jed, who nodded, a wide grin on his face.

"Oh, one more thing," she said. "Alien advice for a better life. Sully – be nice to your mum. And Hutch – " she winked at him – "tell yours that Jed will never forget that special moment he had with her."

Vlak shooed the two of them away, and they took up places either side of the gallery exit, checking one final time to see if they were going to be disturbed. They gave a thumbs-up to Vlak, who then pressed a final button on her wrist and leaned over to hook her arm through Jed's.

A shimmering, bright white circle appeared above their two heads, and lights on the bracelets' onyx bands began to oscillate wildly. There was, remarkably, no noise, just a low whump as the circle extended and then dropped to cover Vlak and Jed where they stood. Jed grinned again, and held his free hand up, fingers splayed, Spock style.

Afterwards – for years, decades – Hutch was never able to understand quite what it was that he and Sully saw next.

For a moment, nothing happened, and then the shimmering circle rose up again around them, like a hula hoop, from their feet to above their heads. As it rose, their bodies shimmered and faded, so that the two of them stood in position, but were first without feet, then legs, then torsos.

The fade was gradual, and as the shimmer passed it seemed to strip away the outer covering of each person.

Hutch first noticed it with Jed, whose trainers and then clothes seemed to melt away, leaving the steadily diminishing outline of a naked human body, which in turn vanished as the circle made its way higher.

Later, it was a tough call, as to which visual picture had been the most disturbing – Jed's middle bits given a starring role as his legs disappeared, or his disembodied grinning head, which was the last thing to wink out.

With Vlak, though, what did he see? Hutch could never quite grasp it, however hard he tried.

First, there was a flash, which he later realised was probably the forcefield that he hadn't really believed in. And then a rolling tumble of folds and pleats, like someone was swirling a curtain – a rippling display of steadily disappearing ribbed limbs in green and yellow, a flat body with a greyish sheen, and an angular head that tilted in a quizzical way. It could have been all that, or perhaps it was nothing but the distortion of the vortex.

And then the circle disappeared, and Vlak and Jed were gone. There was just the display case, now empty, in a silent gallery lined with the stone carvings of another distant civilisation.

Three hours later, the first museum visitors of the day started to wander the halls. Hutch and Sully waited a minute or two, before climbing up and over the rear wall of the Nereid tomb and sidling to the room's exit. The Parthenon Gallery attendant made his way past them, en route to his favourite seat to watch over the famous ancient sculptures and the golden Elgin Bands.

The alarms sounded a few minutes later. As tourists looked around in concern, they were pushed out of the way by a small group of men and women in dark shirts, combats and trainers, who were racing through from the Great Court, down towards the Parthenon Gallery.

Radio chatter from shoulder mikes squawked as they ran, and they took no notice of the two young men who were walking slowly against the tide.

Out through the Great Court they went, down the steps into the museum courtyard, and on out into London, as the sirens got louder.

Chapter 54

BBC World News report:

'The world-famous Elgin Bands in the British Museum have disappeared, presumed stolen, in an incident that Metropolitan Police are calling "baffling."

The priceless golden bracelets – a treasure from the Parthenon on the Acropolis in Athens – have been on display in the British Museum for more than two centuries.

They were discovered to be missing when the museum opened and staff checked the Parthenon Gallery, before the first visitors arrived. The display case was intact, although empty, and the locks had been forced.

According to museum authorities, CCTV coverage in the gallery and in surrounding parts of the museum appears to be incomplete – a "technical malfunction" is being blamed for a temporary loss of power. Technicians are attempting to recover the recordings.

Meanwhile, Metropolitan Police are asking the capital's jewellery shops and auction houses to report any suspicious offers of sale. But for now, significant items from the UK's cultural heritage remain missing – and the Elgin Bands display case at the British Museum is empty for the first time in two hundred years.'

TOP SECRET
Report to: Ministry of Defence, UK Government
By: Director (Europe), Bureau of External Visitor Incursions (BEVI)
Extract from – Case File: Plzeň Incident

'The Plzeň Incident demonstrated the need for a more joined-up approach regarding working with our American counterparts. It's hard to escape the conclusion that – with prior mutual agreement, and more cooperation in the field – we would have retrieved the alien asset (designated 'Matey'), to both our nations' benefits.

Earlier intelligence might also have been gleaned about the importance of the artefacts in the British Museum. It's a matter of major regret that they were in plain sight since initial acquisition in 1816, as their disappearance suggests a strong link to the escape of 'Matey.'

BEVI investigators will continue to assess other likely items in the museum associated with the

Parthenon marbles, but this will take some considerable time.

In the meantime, we urge an approach to US Special Alien Operations for access to Area 51. Plzeň was the single most important visitor insertion in global air space since the 1947 Roswell Incident, and there may well be crossover information and material that would benefit our ongoing investigations.'

———

To: Professor James Storm, Head of Operations, BEVI Research Unit (Germany)
From: Director (Europe), Bureau of External Visitor Incursions (BEVI)

'Jim – you'll have seen the report. Bullshit, mostly, but I did think it was a good opportunity to try and get back to Area 51. You know what they're like about letting us in. Now we've got a near-miss to blame on them, we've got some leverage – for a while at least, anyway.

The craft, though – that stays between us. MoD doesn't know we have it, and neither do the Americans. I gave up those few panels from the forest that you had already scanned, and said they came from an escape pod that we're still examining. When they press to see anything else we might have, I think we'll have had a mysterious electrical fire in the bunker. Destroyed everything, terrible shame.

Sorry we didn't get Matey, Jim – but this could still

turn out to be our Roswell. That craft is going to be the gift that keeps on giving, with any luck. Keep me posted.'

Voice recording, London:

X-Team agent
- Prof? You woke me up. What time is it?

Head of Operations, BEVI Research Unit
[response unavailable]

- Scientists never sleep, is that it?

[response unavailable]

- It's your body, Prof. You've got the chemicals in your lab, you go for it.

[response unavailable]

- Well, bit miffed, if I'm honest. We were so close. You spend your life in this game, you want a result. And while I hate those A-Team wankers, they can at least go and have a look at their little guy in Area 51. I hear he plays a mean game of chess.

[response unavailable]

The Wrong Stop

- Sure, we got the ship, but last I heard it had shut down. Or you'd blown the flux capacitor or something?

[response unavailable]

- I know. I'm always going to be sorry that we didn't get to the museum in time. Bloody gold bangles, I mean, seriously, what kind of tech is that? How was anyone supposed to know that's what they were?

[response unavailable]

- Yeah, maybe we do need someone on the payroll with a history degree? Blows the mind, really, to think they'd been there all that time. Anyway, you've got a lab full of nerds nerding away, if anyone can figure out how to get the ship fired up again, it's you lot. Me, I stick to the running and chasing. And look, lovely chat, Prof, but it's half-past are-you-kidding in the morning.
What's up?

[response unavailable]

- You don't say? Close to home for a change, at least. Probability?

[response unavailable]

- That sounds promising. Wales, though, are you sure?

[response unavailable]

- My experience, Prof, it's hard to find someone in mid-Wales who doesn't claim to be an alien. But ours not to reason why, I'll get the team on it.

[response unavailable]

- You're kidding? How can he stand down those guys? I thought we had carte blanche and a big company credit card?

[response unavailable]

- Yeah, yeah, fiscal responsibility, results-led business, I know. So, you're telling me I have to get up in the middle of the night and drive to Wales on my own to look at some possibly interstellar metal fragments in a farmer's field? They have shotguns, you know? And dogs who can tell you're English.

[response unavailable]

- Don't worry, Prof, I'm up and on it. You know me, I'd do it for free. I bloody love this job.

Chapter 55

Thirty years later:

Corey Hutchinson checked the time, and saw that he had a couple of hours before his train home. The session had finished early, and he'd made his excuses and left. His colleagues were all lovely, but he'd already spent half a day with them poring over Gantt charts and discussing budgets. He thought he could live without '3 to 4pm, Networking and Chat!'

He removed the 'Corey Hutchinson' name badge from his jacket, ducked out of the hotel conference centre, and jumped on an eastbound travelator along Oxford Street.

Now that he was just plain Hutch again, he wondered vaguely about getting off near Soho Square and seeing if any of the old pubs and cafés from his student days were still around. Or maybe he'd wander down to K-Town for a bowl of *chapchae* noodles before the train?

In the end, distracted by the advertising holo-boards, he missed the slide-off exit, and the travelator swung round past the Dominion Theatre ('Ginge Sings! The vintage hits of Ed Sheeran') and headed north up Tottenham Court Road. Hutch slid off at the next exit and stood under a line of palm trees, figuring out his next move.

He could walk to King's Cross-Potterworld from here, but that would only take half an hour, and he really didn't want to wait all that time at the station dodging day-tripper pensioners with broomsticks and flapping scarves.

He crossed over and turned down Great Russell Street almost without thinking. Or maybe not? Perhaps he had always intended to come here?

These days, the accepted theory about free will was that it was an illusion – that whatever you did was a consequence of the immediately preceding thing you did, and so on, for everyone, back to the Big Bang. The thing you did at any point was the *only* thing you could do, given the inexorable, one-way chain of events leading up to it.

If Hutch was now walking along Great Russell Street, then he had always been going to do it today.

As to why? Well, for years Hutch had tried to forget it, and then for several more years – now decades – he scarcely remembered it had happened at all. 'It' being an encounter with an alien called Vlak.

Or if it had happened, then it seemed like it had happened to someone else. The sort of thing you saw in an 'And, finally,' news story. Not the sort of thing, say, you mentioned to your date, then girlfriend, then wife – not if you planned on getting from 'date' to 'wife' anyway.

And that was without the whole, potential rendition-to-a-black-site-dungeon business if anyone ever found out, which meant that forgetting and not-remembering was still very much the way to go, as far as Hutch was concerned. So, thanks very much, unconscious mind and non-free will.

He turned into the British Museum courtyard and cleared the body-scan monitor, which flashed up a cheery 'Have a great day!' and a green tick over the outline image of Hutch's frame.

Another unbidden, fleeting thought about something that had happened a long, long time ago – a full body-scan like that would have scuppered them at the first hurdle.

Inside, Hutch stopped in the soaring Great Court and looked around. He hadn't been here for thirty years, but it seemed very much the same. Different branding, different café, different styles of clothes on different visitors, but recognisably the same space.

As they had left that day, sirens blaring around them, he and Sully had agreed never to go back to the museum.

"You say that like it's a bad thing," Sully had said. "Pub?"

The furore about the missing bracelets dominated the headlines. For days, then weeks, Hutch had expected a tap on the shoulder, a visit from the police, or worse – being thrown into the back of a van by large, unsmiling men in suits and shades. As the weeks stretched into months, it seemed inconceivable that they wouldn't somehow be traced – connected to the event.

They were both interviewed about Jed's disappearance, by the college and by the police. They stuck to their story – that he had come on the train trip around Europe with them, returned home when they did, and then later they'd found his room packed up. No, they'd never seen him again. No, they had no idea what had happened to him, they didn't really know him that well. No, they hadn't known he'd been asked to leave college.

And eventually, miraculously, even that went away. Hutch went from feeling very sick and anxious every day on waking to just feeling a bit sick on some days.

Two more years of college flashed by, and then a move back north. A job, a career, a first date, a wedding, children – by which time, many, many years had passed, and Hutch barely remembered the days when he'd been scared that he would be arrested or snatched every time he set foot outside his door.

He and Sully had drifted apart that second year in college. You'd have thought that encountering an alien from another world together, and helping them escape shadowy forces, might further cement a bond that had existed since childhood. But harbouring a secret they could never talk about, for fear of what might happen, made Hutch and Sully cautious at first – and then they stopped mentioning it at all.

Sully kept going to the pub, Hutch went with him less and less, and when the following summer came round, Sully announced that he was going partying with the rugby boys in Split.

A year later, at the end of his course, Sully got an intern job in the United States, and he'd stayed there pretty much ever since. Married an American girl, settled down. They sent a Christmas card every year.

Funny how you could be so close to someone from the age of seven to twenty and then barely see them for thirty years. There was that non-free will again. Hutch couldn't believe he had *decided* that's how his relationship with Sully was going to go.

He crossed the Great Court and walked through the columned portico to the galleries beyond, pausing at the Rosetta Stone. Still there, still not inscribed upon by aliens, revealing the secrets of the universe, as Jed had wanted to believe.

Jed. Ridiculous Jed.

It wasn't really the alien – Vlak – who Hutch had tried to forget. After all, there wasn't anything he could do with the knowledge that they had met and then helped an alien to escape. Hutch had seen what he had seen, but he couldn't prove anything, and once Sully had drifted away it wasn't like he could talk about it to anyone else.

Jed, though – that was different. Either Jed had gone with Vlak – in which case, it actually was all true, but see above, no proof, could never talk about it – or he hadn't. And if he hadn't, what *had* happened to him? Jed had been big on crazy conspiracy theories, but what kind of mystery could account for everything that had occurred?

At this distance in time, all Hutch could really remember was a circle of shimmering light, a flash and then silence in the empty gallery. Something had happened, but Hutch had never known what, except that the bracelets, Vlak and Jed had all vanished.

Thirty years ago, over three exhausting days, fuelled by alcohol, short of sleep, high on stress, Hutch felt he'd been part of a fever-dream that he'd never been able to explain.

The only proof he had ever had of those events was a photo taken on the platform of Berlin's main station – a selfie, in fact, of Jed standing with Vlak. That Jed had taken using a telescopic selfie stick, which brought back even more half-forgotten memories.

Jed had given him the phone at the last minute, before leaving, and Hutch had destroyed it – but not before taking the photo off and later printing it out. Even at the time, he hadn't been sure why – it later sat in his study drawer, untouched for years.

After all, what did it show? A young man and a young woman, nothing more. One who said she was an alien, and the other who had been mistaken for an alien. Both now gone. Actually, when you looked at it like that, the photo wasn't proof of anything.

Hutch walked on down to the Parthenon Gallery and turned into the main hall. This had changed, but Hutch had known that from the news and TV reports of ten years ago. The Parthenon friezes and sculptures had finally been repatriated to Greece, where they belonged, and the museum had taken the opportunity to remodel the space.

Casts and copies of the decoration of the entire building now stood centre stage, along with holo projections and immersive VR pods that put you right outside the Parthenon of the fourth century BC. It was impressive, Hutch had to admit, and he spent a few minutes reacquainting himself with the history.

They'd even got the original, bright, vibrant colours of the marble columns and statues right, just as Hutch had seen them on Vlak's video-guide – filmed *in situ*, thousands of years ago. What would the museum curators have given to see *that* film?

And there, at one end of the reconstruction, stood an empty case that used to house the golden 'Elgin Bands.' Accompanying text talked of cultural acquisition, and the irony of the famous theft of objects that themselves could have been considered stolen. The empty case, it was said, stood for the careless erasure of history by previous generations – and the hope that, one day, the bracelets would be found and then returned to Greece.

If Hutch was expecting a tingle, a flash – anything – on the site of his most mysterious of life experiences, he was disappointed.

He supposed, in the end, he'd come to make peace with the past. It had finally seemed safe, thirty years later, to return here. No one was after him. He wouldn't be whisked away and interrogated about something he simply couldn't explain.

Hutch would never know exactly what had happened. But that was OK. He touched the empty case and turned for the exit.

———

Before leaving, Hutch ordered a coffee at the café counter in the Great Hall. That prompted another memory – the four of them squeezing into a store cupboard behind the screen at closing time, so that they could hide out overnight. He smiled now, ruefully – what *had* they been thinking?

He found a seat on one of the café benches and checked the time – still an hour before his train, and a twenty-minute walk to the station if he moved quickly.

Hutch sipped his coffee and scanned the Great Hall one last time, and then got up and dropped his cup in a recycling bin. He worked his way through the visitors to the main entrance and then stood for one last time under the grand portico columns, at the top of the steps outside, looking down onto the courtyard.

Someone climbed the steps towards him,

awkwardly catching Hutch's eye and smiling – a young guy in knee-length boardshorts and a T-shirt that said, 'I went outside once, the graphics weren't that good.'

Hutch looked away, checked the time again, and set off down the steps. The guy had stopped halfway up and watched Hutch get closer.

"Hello, Hutch," he said. "Fuck me, you look old."

Chapter 56

Hutch stopped at the sound of his name. He looked at the young bloke – a kid, really. Nineteen, twenty, white ankle socks, loose laces on his Converse All Stars, toting a small, black daypack.

"Do I know – "

"Jed," said the guy. "Seriously, mate? Suppose the eyes go a bit at your age?"

Hutch looked again. There was something about the face – something that grabbed at Hutch's innards and swirled them around. Something that said it was true but also that it couldn't possibly be.

"Jed?" said Hutch. "But – "

"All right, grandad, don't have a heart attack. Here, come and sit down."

Jed moved to the edge of the steps, sat down and patted the floor beside him. Hutch followed suit, never taking his eyes off him.

"Surprise!" said Jed.

Hutch gawped, still searching for something – anything – to say. He looked Jed up and down again. Lean, athletic, bright-eyed, the unblemished face of a nineteen-year-old. Tanned arms, close-cut shorts showing off equally tanned legs.

"Pockets," said Hutch. Not the best opener, but it was all he had in the shock of the moment. "You haven't got any pockets."

"Pockets?" said Jed, grinning. "Where I've been, you don't need pockets."

"*Back to the Future?*" said Hutch, automatically. "Nice," at which he finally rallied. "What I mean is, what the actual – "

"Oh, you mean the age thing?"

"Yes, I mean the age thing! It's been thirty years. Thirty years!"

"Not really," said Jed. "Turns out, time doesn't really work like that."

"What on earth do you mean?"

"It's complicated. Don't worry about it."

"Don't worry? Are you absolutely kidding me right now? Where the hell have you been?"

"Here and there, mate, here and there. Don't you want to know about Vlak?"

"Vlak?" Hutch was feeling this conversation slip away from him by the second.

"You know, hot alien, the hunk from outer space? They're fine, send their regards. They thought it might be a bit much if they turned up as well. I think they were right, you look like you're going to pass out."

"They?"

"It's complicated, a species pronoun thing. I mean, they're all 'they,' though it's not really the right way to think about it. Really, what it is – "

"Jed."

"Yes, mate."

"Shut the fuck up. Please." Hutch looked him up and down again. "God, it really is you?"

"As advertised," said Jed. "Take a minute."

Hutch breathed deeply and looked around. Tourists coming and coming, up and down the steps. A lone policeman sauntering along the courtyard below. A line forming at the ice cream stand.

"How did you get here?" he said, finally. "Tell me you didn't crash a spaceship in London?"

"Next-gen alien tech!" grinned Jed. "Zapped straight in. You remember Arnie in *The Terminator*? Like that, only with my clothes on. It'll be all right, as long as I don't stay too long."

"And how did you know I was here?"

"Please," said Jed. He held out an arm and showed Hutch the oblong smart-help on his wrist. "The things this baby can do. Piece of cake, really."

Hutch touched the device tentatively. No strap, he noticed – it seemed to fit flush on Jed's arm.

"Didn't hurt," said Jed. "More of a tickle. I'm due an upgrade soon, but it's pretty cool. You want to see?"

"No!"

"All right, keep your hair on. What's left of it, anyway. Listen, tell me about Sully. How's he doing? I thought I'd say hello."

"Sully? He's – " Hutch wasn't sure what to say. "He doesn't live here anymore. Hasn't for a long time. He's in America."

"That explains it," said Jed. "Didn't set the parameters wide enough." He tapped his smart-help. "What's he doing out there?"

"Married, kids," said Hutch. "He's a town planner, somewhere in upstate New York."

"Good God. Sully? In charge of planning stuff? Responsible?"

"Yeah, well, we all change. Thirty years is a long time."

"If you say so. God, Sully, I wouldn't have put him in charge of a hamster." Jed shook his head at the thought of Sully working out traffic flows and housing density.

"What are you doing here, Jed? I – we – thought you were dead, or something."

"Not dead. Just travelling. I've seen things you people wouldn't believe."

"*Blade Runner*? Very good."

"Thought you'd like it. But yes, wanted to say hi, hello, how you doing, but also, I've come to give these back."

Jed reached down and unzipped his daypack, and opened the top up so that Hutch could see inside.

Even from deep in the pack, Hutch could see the shine from the two gold bracelets, each with a thinner, darker band.

"Jesus! Close it up! Are you mad?" Hutch looked around wildly, hearing the thunder of feet and the sound of sirens as he imagined chaos descending once again.

"Calm down, no one knows I've got them. Anyway, they're not the real ones – the ones we used. Thanks for all that, by the way. Glad to see you didn't get nabbed and probed. I'd have felt terrible."

"What do you mean, not the real ones? They look exactly like them."

"That's kinda the point, Hutch. I had them made. Right down to the last indent and minor scratch, only these won't ever do anything. They're fakes. Fake wormhole-jump-devices, that is. Not fake bracelets. No one will know the difference."

"Why now? After all this time?"

"I've been meaning to do it, ever since – you know. Nearly came the other week – well, decade, I suppose." Jed looked momentarily disorientated. "Being back here really scrambles my timeline. Anyway, when I saw you'd be here, I thought, kill two birds with one stone."

Hutch shook his head. "I don't know what to do about any of this."

"Nothing for you to do, Hutch, mate. I'm going to

go in there, leave these in a bag on a café table, and you can go about your day. I've written a note, look."

He handed Hutch a piece of paper that said, 'Sorry for taking these. I don't need them anymore, so please take them back. And put some proper locks on the case this time.'

Hutch laughed at that. "They'll be pleased. They never figured it out. Then again, neither did I."

"Turns out," said Jed, "that there are some things that you can't explain, yet apparently they're real." He grinned.

"Looks that way." Hutch paused a moment. "Vlak, she's – they're OK?" He felt strange, asking after someone he'd met for three days, thirty years ago, and still didn't quite know if he believed in.

"They're great. Very funny, though you knew that. And, man, you should meet the family – they really crack me up."

"And you? Are you all right?" That was the question, Hutch realised, that he really wanted an answer to.

"Are you kidding? Living the dream, Hutch, you know me."

Hutch didn't know Jed, though. He never really had. And it had been on his mind for thirty years.

"Only," said Hutch, "I always wanted to say sorry, but never could." He looked Jed in the eye. "I don't think we were very nice to you. Well, Sully was, maybe. I wasn't. And then you were just – gone. It messed with me a bit."

"Don't worry about it," said Jed. "Really. Water under the bridge. Tell you the truth, I wasn't sure about coming away with you back then. Sully, I liked him. You – well, I didn't really know if it would work."

"It did, though, didn't it? We had a good time?"

"Hutch, if you weren't such an organised, anal, by-the-numbers – "

"Steady on."

"Spreadsheet monkey, then we'd have never been on that train, and I'd never have sat next to Vlak. You changed my life. I reckon we're even."

"I think what you're saying is, I'm the hero here?" said Hutch.

"Well, it's – "

"Complicated?"

They both smiled at that.

———

Jed got to his feet and pulled the bag to his shoulder.

"This it?" said Hutch.

"I reckon. Planets to go to, stuff to see. I'm going to go inside the museum and give them their treasures back. Then I'm going to zip off."

"And I've got a train to catch," said Hutch.

"Ah, Earth," said Jed. "You've got to love a land-based, non-quantum transport system."

"Will I see you again?"

"You already have. Here and there. Tell you what, I

wish you'd all hurry up and figure out this time business, it would make all this so much easier."

"I really don't understand."

"And it really doesn't matter. Go live your life, Hutch. Stop worrying. And say hello to your wife."

"How did you – "

"Please." Jed waggled his smart-help at Hutch again.

"Right then."

They stood for a second, facing each other, and then Jed leaned in and hugged him. Hutch felt a slight crackle.

"Forcefield?"

"Couldn't possibly say." Jed stepped away, smiling, gave Hutch the Vulcan hand-wave, and then turned to walk up the steps.

Hutch watched him pass under the columns, at the entrance to the museum. Jed turned once and waved again, and then he disappeared into the swirling crowds.

One second here, the next gone, an echo that reverberated for an instant – or for thirty years.

Hutch made his train with minutes to spare, and slumped into his pre-booked, quiet-coach, forward-facing, window seat. Anal spreadsheet monkey, indeed, he really didn't know what Jed had meant.

It was when he leaned forward to take his jacket off that he discovered the wrapped cloth in his pocket, where Jed must have slipped it. Hutch could feel the hard shapes between his fingers, and didn't have to take the cloth out and unwrap it to know what was in there.

Two hard circles. Bands. Bracelets. He knew they would shine in the afternoon light.

And in his other pocket was a folded sheet of paper, on which Jed had written another note.

Chapter 57

Hutch,

Pockets, you see – useful things, right?

I meant it when I said that there are things out there you'd never believe. The universe is – unbelievable. Extraordinary. I think you'd like it – even the bits you can't explain or put on a spreadsheet.

I'm giving the two copies to the museum, but these bracelets aren't fakes, they're the real deal – pre-programmed for Vlak's home planet. My home planet now. Honestly, you should see it, it's wild.

Give one to Sully, if you ever see him. Or come with your wife. Or give them to your kids (yeah, I checked that, too) – it would be one hell of a summer holiday, better than interrailing, that's for sure, and Uncle Jed would look after them.

You know what to do – press the button on the inside and don't stand near anything flammable. I'll see you when you get here – I'm easy to spot, I'm the only one with one head (kidding!).

Life's been good to me, Hutch, honestly. Come and see us some time. Just don't get off at the wrong stop.

Your friend,

Jed (Galaxy-Master, Space Lord of the Pockets)

―――――

BBC World News report:

'In an extraordinary development, two treasured exhibits that were stolen from the British Museum thirty years ago, have been returned anonymously.

The so-called Elgin Bands – twin gold bracelets from the site of the Parthenon in Athens – disappeared in mysterious circumstances three decades ago. Yesterday, a café assistant found them left in a bag with a note of apology, and turned them over to museum authorities.

The Metropolitan Police have reopened the file on the case. In the meantime, the British Museum has announced that it will place the bracelets on temporary display, back in the Parthenon Gallery. They are expected to be returned to Greece in due course to join the rest of the original finds from the site.'

THE END

―――――

If you enjoyed *The Wrong Stop*, you'll want to grab the **special bonus chapter** that's set right at the end of the book. Who knows where that might lead…?

Just scan the QR code to download the bonus chapter.

Authors' note: story background

Travelling around Europe with an Interrail pass (Eurail for non-Europeans) has been a rite of passage for students and young people since the 1970s. I've done it myself a few times, and my journeys provided the initial inspiration for this book. Not that I ever met an alien, I wish, but I've definitely zipped from country to country, 'doing' major cities in a day, and drinking far too much in the process.

The route the characters follow in the book is entirely do-able, by the way. And there really is a beer spa and a Sex Machines Museum in Prague.

As for the major plot points based around the Parthenon in Athens and the British Museum in London, they are all based on the actual historical record – with one exception.

For details about the construction and use of the Parthenon, I drew upon Professor Mary Beard's brilliantly readable book, *The Parthenon*. In it, she refers to the role of the Treasurers of Athena – as the guardians of Athens' city wealth and gifts – and that gave me the germ of an idea, which became the depositing of Vlak's transporter devices.

Obviously, any mistakes and errors in the Parthenon history, as presented in *The Wrong Stop*, are entirely mine and not the Professor's.

The history regarding Lord Elgin and the Parthenon 'marbles' is well-known, and the sculptural friezes are on display in the British Museum, exactly as described. If you've never seen them, you really should go one day – though there are now more meaningful moves afoot to give the Parthenon sculptures back to Greece, where they would be reunited with the others in Athens' Acropolis Museum.

For now, though, you can still visit the Parthenon sculptures and friezes in the British Museum, and also see the Nereid Monument in the adjacent gallery, where Hutch, Sully, Jed and Vlak hide out. Just to be clear, I don't condone spending the night in the museum after hours, for obvious reasons, whatever Ben Stiller says.

When it comes to the 'Elgin Bands,' though, I'm sorry to disappoint you, but I made them up – as I did the extract from the financial accounts of the Treasurers of Athena of 434 BC, quoted in the prologue and elsewhere. There are many such genuine accounts, some relating to treasures given to the Parthenon, but none that mention gold bracelets (or even alien devices).

That said, the British Museum holds more than four million objects, and if you search the catalogue for 'bracelet,' there are 5,508 results. So I'd like to think that somewhere, either on display or deep in the bowels of the museum, there might well be an extra-terrestrial relic or two, just waiting to be activated.

Like This Book?

If you enjoyed the ride, please take a moment to leave me a review on Amazon, Goodreads, BookBub, or anywhere else you like.

A word or two is absolutely fine (though please, go to town if you like!), and even just a rating makes the book that much more visible to other readers.

Thanks a million – you're all stars.

About the Author

Rex Burke is a SciFi writer based in North Yorkshire, UK.

When he was young, he read every one of those yellow-jacketed Victor Gollancz hardbacks in his local library. That feeling of out-of-this-world amazement has never left him – and keeps him company as he writes his own SciFi adventures.

When Rex is not writing, he travels – one way or another, he'll get to the stars, even if it's just as stardust when his own story is done.

Find Out More

To find out more, and grab a free short story, visit Rex's website – rexburke.com

Made in United States
North Haven, CT
01 September 2024

56668858R00200